Henry Morley

The King and the Commons

Cavalier and Puritan Song

Henry Morley

The King and the Commons
Cavalier and Puritan Song

ISBN/EAN: 9783744742450

Printed in Europe, USA, Canada, Australia, Japan

Cover: Foto ©Andreas Hilbeck / pixelio.de

More available books at **www.hansebooks.com**

THE

KING AND THE COMMONS.

CAVALIER AND PURITAN SONG.

SELECTED AND ARRANGED

BY HENRY MORLEY,

PROFESSOR OF ENGLISH LITERATURE, UNIV. COLL. LOND.

LONDON:

SAMPSON LOW, SON, AND MARSTON.

CROWN BUILDINGS, 188, FLEET STREET.

1868.

CHISWICK PRESS :—PRINTED BY WHITTINGHAM AND WILKINS,
TOOKS COURT, CHANCERY LANE.

INTRODUCTION.

THIS little pleasure-book of English verse attempts to blend the voices of true poets who lived in the time of Charles I. and the Commonwealth, into a genuine expression of the manner of their music and the spirit of their time. During the first seven years of the reign of Charles I. all the poets who are here to be heard singing were alive together. In the next year George Herbert passed away; then Randolph; then, in the middle of the reign, Ben Jonson; Carew next; and in its latter years, besides Quarles and Ford, three died in early manhood—Suckling, Cartwright, and Habington. Drummond's death followed close upon the King's; Crashaw lived only into the next year; Lovelace and Cleveland did not survive the Commonwealth; while Milton and Andrew Marvell, Waller, Davenant, Butler, Denham, Cowley, with George Wither, whose age was sixty at the end of the reign of Charles I., lived on into the time of Charles II. The poems are meant to be so arranged, that while they show the love of song for its own sake, and have for a light background the every-day characters of country life and

town life, mirth of the harvest home, the college, and
the tavern, they do, after striking the keynote with a
few strongly marked pieces, indicate something of the
drift of events to the time of the king's execution,
through verse of his friends. The course of song proceeds, after this, to suggest the spirit of the Commonwealth, and when it has reached the immediate sequel of
the story, closes with the trustful words of Milton, which
our later history has justified. As far as might be,
within limits so narrow, I have tried to give coherence
to a book of extracts, by basing it on the grand story of
our Civil War, and so blending and contrasting the
pieces quoted, sometimes rather for expression of
character than for inherent merit, that they shall speak
the mind of each great party to the struggle as expressed
by its own best men, rather than as caricatured by the
meaner sort of its opponents.

This being the plan of the book, because Cavalier and
Puritan are the only words used generally as short
symbols of the two camps in the great political and
social battle lying at the heart of it, those words are
placed unwillingly, for want of better, on the title-page.
But they have no more specific sense than loose
usage has assigned to them, and are taken as the mere
x and y of a popular algebra. The true division here
intended, and expressed by the chief title of this volume, is between the men who, upon the great questions
of principle then in debate, were with the King, and
those who were with the Commons. Some minds are
so constituted that they combat change, lest they lose
what of truth and right the past has won; others seek
change wherever they believe that they can take part
in the conquests of the future. Minds equal in acuteness are employed continually upon an active test of the

validity of every questionable plea. Truth only is strong enough to live through this incessant questioning; meanwhile the conflict calls forth all the manliness of man. Here, then, there shall be no gathering of narrow spite from anonymous broadsheets. Where there is bitterness,—and that, too, must be shown,—it is the bitterness which conflict bred in men who earned a right to be remembered among wits and poets of their day. These poets, of all parties, had also a sense of brotherhood in their own craft. Party feeling did not blind Wither or Marvell to the genius of Lovelace. A living poet had the living fellowship of his competitors, a dead poet their praise. The lines of Henry Vaughan to a fellow poet (on p. 93), show what was then, and among men of true genius is now, the temper of the craft. A sense of their old comradeship should quicken the enjoyment of this small gathering of the disembodied wit of men who once were glad to come together in the flesh.

Charles Stuart was twenty-five years old when, on the 27th of March, 1625, he came to the throne of England as King Charles I. Ben Jonson, in that year twice as old as King Charles, then occupied the throne of English poetry. He had of late been writing court masques, but for the last nine years he had not written a play for the public stage. It was six years since, in the course of a visit to Scotland, he had spent part of an April month with William Drummond of Hawthornden. Drummond, a man eleven years his junior, left notes of the conversation of his famous guest, which are not altogether creditable to the note-taker. King Ben's long sickness began with a stroke of palsy in the year of the accession of King Charles. He wrote again for the theatre because he needed bread; wrote the "Staple of

News," and the "New Inn," received ungenerously, though its epilogue said of it, "the maker is sick and sad." This caused him to write the indignant verses which, with a few lines in recognition of a gift from Charles, represent in this little book the painful close of an old master's life among the men of the new generation. The true wits of the day paid Ben Jonson utmost honour; none more cordially than the best of the young men who pleased the court of Charles. They were Ben's courtiers too, and lived with the better of their sovereigns in kindly fellowship.

"My son Cartwright writes all like a man," said Jonson. Cartwright was but fourteen years old at the accession of King Charles, and but six-and-twenty when Ben Jonson died. He was one of those who died, as has been said, before the reign was out, when he had scarcely ripened into man's estate. Yet he had indeed written and worked like a man. He earned repute at Oxford as a scholar with the gift of genius, went into holy orders at the age of twenty-seven, and leapt into fame as "a most florid and seraphical preacher." His loyalty to the king and appetite for work,—he is said to have studied sixteen hours a day,—caused him to be made by his University one of the council of war to provide for the king's troops sent to protect the colleges. He was imprisoned when the forces of the Parliament prevailed at Oxford, but released on bail. William Cartwright not only wrote some of the best poems and plays of his time, and preached some of the best sermons, but as reader of metaphysics in his University he earned especial praise. King Charles wore black on the day of his funeral, and fifty wits and poets of the time supplied their tributary verses to the volume, first published in 1651, of "Comedies, Tragi-Comedies, with other Poems, by Mr. William Cartwright, late Student of Christ Church in Oxford, and Proctor of the University. The Airs and Songs set by Mr. Henry Lawes." There is in this book a touching portrait of young Cartwright, evidently a true likeness, with two rows of books over his head, and his elbow upon the open volume of Aristotle's metaphysics. He rests on his hand a young head, in which the full under-lip and downy beard are harmonized to a face made spiritual by intensity of thought. Cartwright died, in his thirty-second year, of a camp fever that killed many in Oxford. These pages include a Lullaby, from his tragi-comedy of the Siege, or Love's Convert; the rest of the pieces representing him are independent poems.

Another of those short-lived men who yet survive as poets was Thomas Randolph, twenty years old at the accession of King Charles. He too was counted by Ben Jonson in the number of his sons. He was of Westminster School and Cambridge University, before he lived too fast among the wits of town as play writer and poet. Staphyla's Lullaby, given in these pages, as burlesque pendant to the lullaby of Cartwright's is from Randolph's "Jealous Lovers," and the dainty fairy jingle at p. 65 is from " Amyntas." The language of these fairies, who come from the moon, is not English; but they say only that they are very small, that they like apples and rob orchards at night, because stolen fruit is sweetest.

William Habington, whose age was twenty at His Majesty's accession, was of a Roman Catholic family in Worcestershire, the son of a studious man who got materials together for a history of his own county, when, instead of death punishment he was condemned to stay for life in Worcestershire, because he had concealed in his house persons implicated in the gunpowder plot. William Habington was educated at St. Omer by the Jesuits, but declined to become one of their order. He came home, and expressed the pure delights of love and marriage in a series of poems, his " Castara," first published in 1635, and revised in 1640. Habington's Castara was the lady whom he married,—Lucy, daughter of William Herbert, the first Lord Powis. He wrote also a tragi-comedy, " The Queen of Arragon," which was acted and published in 1640 by the King's Chamberlain, without consent of its author. The song in this volume, entitled " Young Folly," belongs to the fourth act of the play ; the other pieces of his are all from " Castara." Habington took no active part in politics, but was of the king's friends, and wrote a " History of Edward IV." at his majesty's desire.

Sir John Suckling, son of the Comptroller of the Royal Household, was a year younger than Milton,— he being sixteen, Milton seventeen, at the date of the accession of Charles I.; and he died seven or eight years before the king. He was the lively son of a grave father, who qualified him to speak Latin at the age of five. Suckling made, in his youth, the tour of the Continent, fought in the army of Gustavus Adolphus, lived expensively in London with the poets for his friends, and raised for the king's service a troop of horse. Some have it that his death was hastened by mortification of heart, because his men ran from the Scots after he had spent £12,000 upon their gay equipment. Others say it was mortification of the heel, caused by a penknife or rusty nail which his valet de chambre, before robbing him, put in his boot to stay pursuit.

Richard Crashaw was of about Suckling's age. He was, like Cartwright, a popular enthusiastic preacher at

Oxford as well as a poet; was expelled from Oxford by the parliamentary army, went to France, became a devout Roman Catholic, and suffered much distress till the good offices of the Queen obtained for him employment at Rome, where he died of a fever in 1650.

Edmund Waller was about four years older than Suckling and Crashaw, and of the same age as Habington. His mother was John Hampden's sister, but a strong royalist, and as his father died when Edmund Waller was an infant, leaving him a large fortune, it was she who sent him to Eton and to Cambridge. He married a great heiress who died young, and left him, a rich widower of five-and-twenty, to pay unsuccessful court to the Lady Dorothea Sidney, whom he celebrated in his verse as Sacharissa. His Amoret is said to have been Lady Sophia Murray. Waller began his political career with his uncle Hampden's party; was arrested and narrowly escaped with his life for plotting against the Commons. Under the Commonwealth he wrote a panegyric on Cromwell; and the Restoration made him flatterer of Charles the Second.

Probably of the same age as Waller, but a stauncher man, was John Cleveland, the son of a Leicestershire vicar. He was for nine years a Fellow of St. John's College, Cambridge, in repute at the University as orator and poet. Deprived of his Fellowship as one of the first who, at the outbreak of the Civil War, spent his best wit in the king's service, Cleveland betook himself to the king's head-quarters at Oxford. Afterwards, with the garrison at Newark-on-Trent, he served as Judge Advocate, and most unwillingly obeyed the king's order to surrender. He then became a prisoner at Yarmouth, and was in great misery until, upon representation of his suffering, he was set free by Cromwell;

whom, after this, it was a point of honour with him not to attack. Cleveland abstained for the rest of his days from politics, and died of fever in 1659.

Sir William Davenant also was of Waller's age, born in the same year, 1605. His father was an Oxford inn-keeper, but he was willing to be thought a natural son of Shakespeare. He made his first appearance at court as page to a duchess, and pleased both court and town so well with his plays, that on the death of Ben Jonson the Queen procured Davenant's succession to the post of laureate. In the following year he was appointed governor of the king and queen's company of actors at the Cockpit in Drury Lane. He ran great risks for the king's cause in the Civil War, and was knighted for his services at the siege of Gloucester. The queen employed him as a confidential agent. Afterwards, when a prisoner in Cowes Castle he finished his six cantos of Gondibert, and under the Commonwealth it is said that he owed his safety to the good offices of Milton. Obtaining freedom, he contrived under the Commonwealth to evade the interdict on plays; and the Restoration brought him to great honour as a playhouse manager.

Samuel Butler, who wrote his "Hudibras" in the Restoration days, was thirteen years old at the accession of Charles I. He was three years older than Sir John Denham, and six years older than Lovelace and Cowley. He was a poor man always, and in some part of the time of Charles I. had an office in the family of the Countess of Kent, from whose library, perhaps, he derived some of his learning.

Sir John Denham, the son of an Irish Chief Baron, studied law as well as a propensity for gambling would permit. After his father's death he gambled away part of his inheritance, and was hardly suspected of poetry until in 1642 he produced his play of the "Sophy," wherewith Waller said that he "broke out like the Irish Rebellion, threescore thousand strong, when nobody was aware or in the least suspected it." The queen trusted him in 1647 with a message to the king, and he was employed afterwards with Cowley in carrying on the king's correspondence. Under the Commonwealth he was a ruined man; but Charles II. made him a Knight of the Bath and surveyor of the king's buildings.

Lovelace and Cowley, both born in the same year, 1618, were seven years old at the accession of Charles I.

Richard, eldest son of Sir William Lovelace, at sixteen was the handsomest gentleman commoner in Oxford. He was made M.A. of his university at the request of a great lady who admired his beauty; went to court; served with the army in the north as ensign and as captain. For presenting a Kentish petition on the king's behalf, Lovelace was committed to the Gatehouse at Westminster, where he wrote his song "To Althea from Prison," and after three or four months' confinement was released only upon heavy bail. He spent much of his fortune in the service of the king, and the relief of men of genius who fell into distress. His "Lucasta" was Lucy Sacheverell, who, upon a false report of his death from wounds received at Dunkirk, married another of her suitors. In the last months of the life of Charles I. Lovelace was again a prisoner in London, solacing himself with poetry. He was released after the execution of the king, when the fine hearted Cavalier poet ended his days under the Commonwealth in years of extreme misery and want. He died in an alley near Shoe Lane.

Cowley, a grocer's son, left early to the sole care of

his mother, poet as a boy and growing up into the largest poetical reputation of a later time, was so heartily the king's friend that in the last years of the great struggle he was chiefly trusted with the ciphering and deciphering of the royal correspondence; and in him one of the most fanciful of our poets proved himself to be very practical as a man of business.

Sir Edward Sherburne, too, was born in the year 1618. He succeeded his father as clerk of the ordnance in 1641, but was rejected for his adherence to the king. He fought at Edgehill, and was made master of arts when with the king at Oxford. He survived till 1702.

Alexander Brome, two years younger than Lovelace and Cowley, was an attorney turned song writer, who supplied a chief part of the loyal minstrelsy with which the king's friends graced their cups, and boldly used his pen under the Commonwealth in aid of a restoration of the Monarchy. His gayer strains answered their purpose, and there is a poem of his in this volume (p. 103) which shows an underlying earnestness of character.

Among the elder men blending their voices with these representatives of the generation that fought out the Civil War is George Sandys, born when Shakespeare was a boy of thirteen. George Sandys was the seventh son of an archbishop, and in the seventh year of Charles I. he published that paraphrase of the Psalms from which we take a strain at the close of the first part of this volume.

George Herbert was sixteen years younger than Sandys. Under James I. George Herbert looked for court patronage and hoped to be a Secretary of State. The death of James destroyed this hope, and on the accession of King Charles he devoted himself to religion. To this reign, then, belongs the memorable part of

Herbert's life spent in his parsonage at Bemerton, the purest upholder of that principle of church authority which went side by side with maintenance of the divine right of kings.

Another clergyman was Robert Herrick, who was of George Herbert's age, or about two years older; but Herbert died of consumption in the eighth year of the reign of Charles I., while Herrick lived through the Commonwealth into the time of Charles II. In 1629, King Charles I. presented Herrick to the Vicarage of Dean Prior, in what he calls "dull Devonshire." There he lived and preached inaudible sermons; a bachelor poet with a tame pig for his pet, and a maid Prue to take care of him. He professed to be glad when the Parliament, in 1648, deprived him of his vicarage, and obliged him to come to London; where he would have starved had not his poems made him friends. At the Restoration Herrick got his vicarage again, and he survived till 1674.

Thomas Carew, who was born nearly in the same year with Herrick, had a shorter life. Being of an old Devonshire family, he perhaps would not have agreed that Devonshire was dull; but he spent little time there. He was lively and gay, enjoying the best pleasures of the town, which Herrick sighed for. He was gentleman of the privy chamber and sewer in ordinary to King Charles I., and one of the inner circle also in Ben Jonson's court. He is said to have died two years after Jonson.

Francis Quarles was but a few months older than George Herbert. Cambridge was his university. He had been cupbearer to King James's daughter, and afterwards secretary to Archbishop Usher until the rebellion of 1641 drove him from Ireland. Among his works,—" The Emblems" are still popular,—was a pamphlet called "The Loyal Convert," ascribed also to Dr. H. Hammond, written at the outset of the Civil War. When Quarles afterwards joined the king at Oxford, he lost his property, including books and MSS., and his death, which occurred in 1644, is said to have been hastened by his troubles. As there is no verse of his in the following pages, he shall be represented here by a few lines out of " The Invocation," before his " Divine Poems ":—

> O All-sufficient God, great Lord of Light,
> Without whose gracious aid, and constant sprite,
> No labours prosper, howsoe'er begun;
> But fly like mists before the morning sun:
> O raise my thoughts, and clear my apprehension,
> Infuse thy spirit into my weak invention:
> Reflect thy beams upon my feeble eyes,
> Shew me the mirror of thy mysteries;
> My artless hand, my humble heart inspire,
> Inflame my frozen tongue with holy fire:
> Ravish my stupid senses with thy glory;
> Sweeten my lips with sacred oratory:
> And thou, O First and Last, assist my quill,
> That first and last I may perform thy Will.
> My sole intent's to blazon forth thy praise;
> My ruder pen expects no crown of bays.
> Suffice it then thine altar I have kist:
> Crown me with glory: take the bays that list.

William Drummond of Hawthornden, whom Jonson had visited in Scotland, enjoyed literary ease on his paternal estate, before he travelled abroad for eight years, then coming home into the midst of civil war, sought quiet in the society of his brother-in-law, Sir John Scot of Scotstarvet. For his writings as a royalist the Commons fined him heavily in men and arms wherewith to fight against the cause he sang for. His estates lying in three counties, he considered that the men were claimed of him in fractions, and wrote thereupon :

"Of all these forces raised against the King,
Tis my strange hap not one whole man to bring;
From divers parishes get divers men,
But all in halfs and quarters; great king, then
In halfs and quarters if they come 'gainst thee,
In halfs and quarters send them back to me."

John Ford, the dramatist, was but a few months younger than Drummond.   He wrote to please himself, not rapidly; and though allied to the great company of the Elizabethan dramatists, his best plays were produced in the reign of Charles I.   We have here only a dirge from his play of the "Broken Heart."

James Shirley, who is said to have died of the shock he suffered in the Fire of London, was ten years younger than Ford.   He had a curacy in the Church of England, but having joined the Church of Rome, opened a school at St. Albans.   Then he came to London and wrote plays, obtained the good will of the Queen, and went to Ireland for a year with the Earl of Kildare.   In the Civil War he fought under the lead of his patron the Earl of Newcastle.   Under the Commonwealth, when he might not write plays, he kept school again, and wrote "Rudiments of Grammar."   The verses of his here given are from "The Contention of Ajax and Ulysses."

Barten Holiday was an archdeacon of Oxford, who wrote sermons, and translated Juvenal and Persius. The Tobacco song which he contributes to this volume is from an allegorical play called "Technotamia, or the Marriage of the Arts."

Jasper Mayne was also a divine, and he was deprived

of his studentship of Christ Church for writing an " Och-
lomachia, or the People's War examined according to
the principles of Scripture and Reason." He was a
lively man, who had then written two plays, from one of
which—" The Amazon's War "—there is here a song of
the passing away of Time, which is the strophe of a
song sung by two Amazons, having an antistrophe which
answers to its measure line for line.

Thomas Heywood, from whom we take a " Love's
Good Morrow," was a veteran playwright, said to have
been concerned in two hundred and twenty dramatic
pieces, of which twenty-three are printed. He was a
Lincolnshire man and Fellow of Peterhouse; at the
close of Elizabeth's reign a regular actor, and sharer in
Henslowe's company ; and in the time of Charles I., one
of the theatrical servants of the Earl of Worcester.

Samuel Rowley was a player and dramatist of less
mark, from whose " Noble Spanish Soldier," we have
here a song of Sorrow.

Richard Brathwaite, born about 1588, at Kendal, in
Westmoreland, was educated at Oriel College, Oxford,
lived upon his freehold, was a deputy-lieutenant and
justice of the peace in Westmoreland, married twice,
had by his first wife six sons and three daughters, and
wrote much in prose and verse, with sharp antagonism
to the Puritans.

King Charles himself is among the singers ; for although his authorship of the verses said to have been
written by him at Carisbrook may fairly be doubted,
they are in these pages assigned to him as usual. Small
as our selection is, it contains pieces by more than thirty
writers who represent the side of the court, although
but three,—Wither, Marvell, and Milton,—who speak
for the people.

George Wither, born in 1588, came from Magdalen College, Oxford, to enter himself of Lincoln's Inn. The examples here given of his verse express his religious sturdiness of character. In 1639 he was a captain of horse in the expedition against the Scots; but in the Civil War he raised a troop for the Parliament by selling his estate. To royal ears his verse appeared libellous before the days of Charles I., and after the days of the Commonwealth. We may here see for ourselves the temper of his libelling.

Andrew Marvell was but a young man in the time of Charles I., and made his chief mark as a satirist of Charles II. and his court. In the time of Charles I. he was tutor to the daughter of Fairfax, and under the Commonwealth assisted Milton in his office of Latin secretary to the Protector.

Milton, seventeen years old at the accession of Charles I. wrote in his reign "Comus," "Lycidas," "L'Allegro," and "Il Penseroso," with other poems which belong to a distinct epoch in his life; the period of his prose works, that is to say of his active participation in the public life of his own day, intervening. The true poet either leads or follows his time; perhaps there was a hint of this in the form of Ben Jonson's welcome to the Oracle of Apollo; but whether he lead or follow, it is with his time that he will march. There are solitudes of genius, but the outward isolation of the greatest poet is not unlike that of a great captain with serried armies at his back, who is, at heart, of all men in his armies the least isolated, since his mind is the one most occupied with care for all. We think of a Dante with something of the sense which caused Wordsworth to say of Milton that his soul was like a star and dwelt apart; but there is not a poet in all literature, follower or leader, whose verse is more thoroughly than Dante's, soul and body of the time for which it was created. Milton put off his singing robes to labour for the State, and between the springtime of his genius and the glorious harvest of its autumn, gave the summer of his life to direct service of the country. His was then the pen of the Commonwealth, the voice of England to the outer world. And in his earlier and later verse, not less than in the middle period of his prose writing, Milton's genius was rich with the life of his own time, although he thought apart from the crowd, and spoke for himself, royally, with independent power. No poet is for all time who is not also for his age, reflecting little or much of its outward manner, but a part of its best mind.

In the world of intellect, varieties of form and use and stature are as infinite as in the world of animals or plants. Cedar and violet depend for sustenance upon the common earth; and poets of all forms and fashions draw their life out of the common world of thought from which they spring. Varieties of intellectual soil, changes of climate or of season, local accidents of sun and shade, determine for each place and time what forms of thought shall spring up and flourish, what shall wither without bearing seed. If the estimation of our great writers were not upheld strongly by tradition, and verified from time to time by critical appreciation among those who join a sense of poetry with leisure for the study necessary to enable them to read each author as a contemporary would have read him, much of our best literature would have become extinct. 1647, 1747, 1847, each has its own accidents of taste. The first appearance, in 1847, of a piece written to the taste of men's minds at either of the other dates would be as little appreciated as the entrance of a visitor in a large frilled collar or a periwig. Happily, dress is not all. A well-marked individuality distinguishes the work of every man with a spark of genius in his nature. This individuality, I think, is distinct in a poem by Milton, which is here printed for the first time in any volume. It stands in what I believe to be the handwriting of Milton himself, on a blank page in the volume of "Poems both English and Latin," which contains his "Comus," "Lycidas," "L'Allegro," and " Il Penseroso." It is signed, I believe, with his initials, and dated December, 1647. It was discovered in this manner:—In arranging the pieces contained in this volume I desired to quote, as far as possible, the author's copies. Misprints creep in, and editors take liberties now and then. For example, even so sound an English scholar as the late Robert Bell overlooked in his collection of " Songs of the Dramatists," misprints in the last two lines of Barten Holiday's Tobacco song (see p. 67), which transformed them into

> He's the wiser that does drink;
> Thus armed I fear not a Fury.

Or again, George Wither's " Shall I Wasting in Despair," and his " Hence away, ye Sirens leave me," first printed in a volume of Wither's " Workes," which the author disclaimed, are seldom given without some or all of the variations which he most expressly and emphatically repudiated. Desiring to represent faithfully the authors here quoted,[1] where I did not myself possess ori-

---

[1] I have also avoided the common practice, of quoting abridged pieces as if they were complete, and, unless the piece is distinctly given as an extract, show in the margin (using the abridgments *st.*, *ll.* and *w.*) where stanzas or lines have been omitted, and how many; also in the two instances where words

c

ginal editions of their works to quote from, I looked for
them in the reading-room of the British Museum. For-
tunately, it did not seem to me useless to read a proof
containing passages from Milton with help of the original
edition of his English and Latin poems published in
1645. There are two copies of that book in the Museum
—one in the General Library, which would be the one
commonly consulted, and the other in the noble collection formed by George III., known as the King's Library,
which was the copy I referred to. The volume, which
has been rebound since the epitaph was written in it,
and has lost, therefore, the original fly leaves, contains
first the English, then the Latin poems of that first
period of Milton's life, each separately paged. The
Latin poems end on page 87, leaving the reverse of the
leaf blank; and this blank I found covered with handwriting, which I took to be the handwriting of John
Milton. It proved to be a transcript of a poem in fifty-
four lines entitled simply "An Epitaph," and signed, I
think, though the first letter of the signature being
much faded and obliterated by the Museum stamp,
which covers it, is open to some doubt, "J. M., 10ᵇᵉʳ.
1647." Milton was in that month 39 years old. As the
page is about the size of a leaf of note paper, the handwriting is small. Thirty-six lines were first written, which
filled the left-hand side of the page, then a line was
lightly drawn to the right of them, and, the book being
turned sideways, the rest of the poem was packed into
three little columns, eight lines in each of the first two

---

have been changed, the number of words altered. One or two
long poems by Wither, given as extracts, are meant to represent
the spirit of his work in an epitome, by bringing together its
most characteristic lines.

columns, and the other two lines at the top of the third column, followed by the initials and date. Upon the small blank space left in this corner of the page the Museum stamp is affixed, covering the faded first letter of what I hold to be Milton's signature. The following copy of the poem has the MS. contractions expanded, and the spelling modernised; but on the blank leaf at the end of this volume it is printed just as it is written on the blank leaf at the end of Milton's book. A facsimile of the page itself is also given as the best aid to a settlement of the disputed question of handwriting. The subject of the poem is the germ of immortality within the dust to which man has returned :—

An Epitaph.

He whom heaven did call away
Out of this Hermitage of clay
Has left some reliques in this Urn
As a pledge of his return.

Meanwhile the Muses do deplore
The loss of this their paramour,
With whom he sported ere the day
Budded forth its tender ray.
And now Apollo leaves his lays
And puts on cypress for his bays;
The sacred sisters tune their quills
Only to the blubbering rills,
And while his doom they think upon
Make their own tears their Helicon;
Leaving the two-topt Mount divine
To turn votaries to his shrine.

Think not, reader, me less blest,
Sleeping in this narrow chest,
Than if my ashes did lie hid
Under some stately pyramid.
If a rich tomb makes happy, then
That Bee was happier far than men,

Who, busy in the thymy wood,
Was fettered by the golden flood,
Which from the Amber-weeping tree
Distilleth down so plenteously;
For so this little wanton elf
Most gloriously enshrined itself.
A tomb whose beauty might compare
With Cleopatra's sepulchre.

In this little bed my dust
Incurtained round I here intrust;
While my more pure and nobler part
Lies entomb'd in every heart.

Then pass on gently, ye that mourn,
Touch not this mine hollowed Urn;
These Ashes which do here remain
A vital tincture still retain;
A seminal form within the deeps
Of this little chaos sleeps;
The thread of life untwisted is
Into its first consistencies;
Infant nature cradled here
In its principles appear;
This plant thus calcined into dust
In its Ashes rest it must
Until sweet Psyche shall inspire
A softening and prolific fire,
And in her fostering arms enfold
This heavy and this earthy mould.
Then as I am I'll be no more
But bloom and blossom [as] bef[ore]
When this cold numbness shall retreat
By a more than chymick heat.

[J.] M., 10ber, 1647.

When I first read these verses, I felt that Milton spoke
through them, with his own mind in his own manner.
The Epitaph was not one of his finished masterpieces,
but had touches worthy of him, and the date suggested
at once an occasion upon which it might be written.

After giving a few days to the consideration of the poem, I took counsel upon the question of matter and style, apart from handwriting, with Mr. John Forster, the friend upon whose sound judgment in all questions of literary criticism I have been accustomed to rely, and whose opinion in this case would be the best attainable; for the author of the life of Goldsmith, and of the masterly essays upon Steele, Defoe, and Churchill, as well as of the best studies of the Civil War time yet given to English literature, while second to none among men of letters as a literary critic, is of chief authority in questions which concern the history and literature of the time of Charles I. and the Commonwealth. With Mr. Forster, then, I left a copy of the Epitaph, and when I saw him next found that he had not a shadow of doubt as to the authorship. And whether autograph or copy, or whatever its history, it surely is a piece of Milton—of Milton not at his best, nor at his worst, but with his grandeur of thought, and written as he only could have written it. The book now in the reader's hand contains a fair general representation of the writing of the other poets who lived at the same time. To some extent, therefore, he can here learn to distinguish by comparison the tone of Milton's voice among the company of singers.

It was by Mr. Forster's advice that the poem thus found was submitted at once to the sharpest test by publication in the *Times*. The question so put excited and is still exciting a degree of interest which makes it necessary that the record of the controversy raised upon it should be more full than otherwise would be consistent with the due proportion of parts in a little book like this. A noble lord who has written verse became the mouthpiece of those who declared that Milton's au-

thorship of the poem was disproved by internal evidence.
I am very much indebted to Lord Winchilsea for the
courage and good humour with which he has expressed
nearly all possible doubts of this description. The
greater number of his arguments from internal evidence were at once met by writers of a contrary opinion ;
and if, to show the complete strength of the case for
Milton's authorship of the Epitaph, I take in succession
all Lord Winchilsea's objections to it, and, either directly
or by inference, include every other objection that I
have seen urged, I must often repeat what has already
been said more effectively by others. But that part of
the reply which consists only in recapitulation is hardly
to be separated from the rest without leaving upon some
readers the impression that, after all, upon some point
or other, some unanswerable difficulty may have been
somewhere raised. I will go through these arguments
from manner as briefly as I can, for I wish also to say a
few words on the matter of the poem, and then add a
remark or two upon the handwriting.

Lord Winchilsea objects to rhyme and sentiment in
the lines :—

" Meanwhile the Muses do deplore,
  The loss of this, their paramour."

In the hymn on Christ's Nativity Milton says of
nature—

" It was no season, then, for her,
  To wanton with the sun, her lusty paramour."

Here the word has a worse rhyme. Lord Winchilsea
seems to have forgotten the original sense of a word
kindred to the old French *paraimer*, to love greatly.
Paramour meant the best-beloved, or, as it is Latinised
in the *Promptorium Parvulorum, preamatus.* Ben Jonson,
writing in the reign of Charles I., to which the epitaph

belongs, makes it the last word in his " Masque of Chlo-
ridia," the crowning compliment to Anne of Denmark,
that she is " the top of paramours."

Lord Winchilsea objects to the beautiful metaphor,—

> " Ere the day
> Budded forth its tender ray,"

as overstrained. Had the new poem happened to be
L'Allegro the same objection might have been made to
the sun's rising in state,

> " Robed in flames and amber light,
> The clouds in thousand liveries dight."

Or had it been *Il Penseroso*, what would have been said
of a "civil-suited morn,"

> " Not trick'd and frounc'd as she was wont
> With the Attic boy to hunt,
> But kercheft in a comely cloud."

Lord Winchilsea's next objection is that he has heard
of porcupine quills and goose quills, but never of quills
as the poet's reeds. Yet reed is the first sense of the
word quill; derived, as we are taught at school, from
calamus, or caulis, and so used by Milton when he
writes,

> " The sacred sisters tune their quills
> Only to the blubbering rills."

Milton has used the word also in *Lycidas :*—

> " He touched the tender stops of various quills;"

and Spenser writes,

> " To sadder times thou may'st attune thy quill."

" Blubbering" is a word of which the sense in Milton's
time was not degraded. It had been first taken from
the rills to be applied to a face swollen with weeping ;
its original sense being drawn from, or closely associated
with, the bubbling of a swollen stream. They still say in

Northamptonshire, next county to that in which Milton wrote his early poems, "the water blubbers up," and Palsgrave's French Dictionary explains " *Blober* upon water" by *bouteillis.*   Thence came the image of a face swollen with tears. Sir Philip Sidney wrote, " Fair streams represent unto me my blubbered face." Spenser used the word always seriously ; and Milton here carries the imitative sound back as an epithet for the rills whence it was taken, with the sense of human grief attached to it.

Lord Winchilsea's next objection is to the phrase " turn votaries to his shrine ;" he would have " votaries at." But a votary is one devoted ; people " turn " to and are not said to be " devoted at " anything.   So Shakespeare wrote " a votary to fond desire."

The next objection is to the amber-weeping tree, which

> " Distilleth down so plenteously."

Lord Winchilsea utterly denies that Milton would have used such a word as "plenteously."   In *Paradise Lost* he uses it, and there, also, with emphasis, to close a line :—

> " which plenteously
> The waters generated by their kinds."

As to rhyme, "tree" is as fairly linked with " plenteously" in this Epitaph as with " cruelty" in the Epitaph on the Marchioness of Winchester.

Lord Winchilsea objects to the rhyme—

> " A tomb whose beauty might compare
> With Cleopatra's sepulchre."

But it is obvious that the intellectual music would have been destroyed had Milton not preferred an assonance to a true rhyme, which would have forced emphasis upon the last syllable of the word sepul*chre.*

Lord Winchilsea objects to the voice from the tomb which speaks of the soul as "my more pure and nobler part." Any reader may, by trial of other possible methods of expression, discover for himself that the best emphasis is obtained by repeating and varying the form that expresses the soul's exaltation ; so varying it also as to give simple force to the word "pure," which is a characteristic epithet more frequent in the works of Milton than, I believe, in those of any other English poet. Indeed, the two epithets here linked are precisely those which elsewhere we find applied by Milton to the definition of the soul. In *Paradise Lost* (Bk. X., l. 784) he calls it "that *pure* breath of life, the spirit of man ;" and in *Paradise Regained* (Bk. II. l. 477),

> " The soul
> Governs the inner man, the *nobler part*."

Lord Winchilsea next objects to the rhyme "mourn" and urn. Precisely this rhyme occurs in a passage of *Lycidas*, which also disposes of another of Lord Winchilsea's objections, that Milton could not (although Shakespeare did in the *Midsummer Night's Dream*[1]) represent thyme as growing in a wood :—

> " Now thou art gone and never must return !
> Thee, shepherd, thee the woods and desert caves,
> With wild thyme and the gadding vine o'ergrown,
> And all their echoes mourn."

The same rhyme occurs also in *Samson Agonistes*.

As to the matter of fact concerning wild thyme, I may add that it often abounds in hilly woodlands in the short open greensward between the trees ; and I am told, as an instance of this, that the upper Cranham woods,

---

[1] And Horace too :
> " Tutum per nemus arbutos
> Quærunt latentes et thyma."—*Od.* I. xvii.

near Birdlip, Gloucestershire, now contain some of the finest banks of wild thyme in the county.

The real defect of grammar in the lines,

> " Infant nature cradled here
> In its principles appear,"

suggests to Lord Winchilsea that Milton was incapable of such oversights.   Every student knows that, even in their finished works as published by themselves, not many of our old authors are free from them ; and that one feature of Bentley's edition of *Paradise Lost* was an absurd attempt to rectify the poet's grammar, some- times in passages where there was really a defect, sometimes where the defect was in Bentley's own sense of the language of poetry.   Had *Lycidas* been the poem newly-found, Lord Winchilsea might have been shocked to find, within the first seven or eight lines, that the author had not been particular enough about the agreement of his verb with his nominatives :—

> " Bitter constraint and sad occasion dear
> Compels me to disturb your season due."

And he may doubt Milton's authorship of *Comus* when he learns that this poem also confounds singular and plural in speaking of—

> " *Those* thick and gloomy *shadows* damp,
> Oft seen in charnel vaults and sepulchres,
> Lingering and sitting by a new made grave,
> As loth to leave the body that *it* loved."

The last twelve lines are nonsense to Lord Winchelsea. That statement involves a question not of style, but of the purport and sense of the whole poem, to which I will turn presently.   To every one of Lord Winchilsea's instances of difference between the style of the Epitaph and Milton's way of writing, the reply, it will be seen, is of a kind more or less strongly confirming the opinion

I have ventured to express, that the new poem is in Milton's manner.

Another critic has found difficulty in believing that so good a scholar as Milton could have confounded Helicon, the mountain, with its fountains, Aganippe and Hippocrene, as the author of the Epitaph appears to have done in saying that the sacred sisters, while they think upon the doom of their lost friend, " Make their own tears their Helicon." Helicon, famed for its abundant waters, was very commonly used, by Metonym, before Milton to represent them. It is one of the most frequent forms of trope to put the container for the thing contained, " ex eo quod continet, id quod continetur," as Quintilian expressed it. Thus, Helicon passed into poetry as a name for all its waters. Spenser who, like Milton, was a scholar, and delighted in the adornment of his verse with thoughts from the old Latin and modern Italian writers, transferred the name of the mountain to its streams much more distinctly than it is here done, or even in Milton's Latin poem on the death of the Vice-Chancellor mourned " mediis Helicon in undis," when, fresh from College, he wrote in the *Shepherd's Calendar,*—

> " And eke you Virgins that on Parnasse dwell,
> *Whence floweth Helicon, the learned well,*
> Help me to blaze
> Her worthy praise
> Which in her sex doth all excel."

And Spenser, it may be remembered, was Milton's favourite poet. " Milton," wrote Dryden in the preface to his *Fables,* " was the poetical son of Spenser. . . . Milton has acknowledged to me that Spenser was his original."

Upon this point let me add what has been written to

me by Dean Stanley, who is well acquainted with the scenery of Greece:—

"There are two special reasons for Milton's employing a general instead of a specific name for the springs of Helicon. One is the fact that as there are two sacred springs there, Aganippe and Hippocrene, Helicon is the only name which covers both. The other is that under no circumstances could the more famous of the two names, Aganippe, and with difficulty the less famous, Hippocrene, come into the verse. 'Leaving the two-topt Mount divine' is Milton all over. 'With hollow shriek the steep of Delphos leaving' is used of the same locality. The allusion to the two cliffs of Parnassus is in exact accordance with that familiarity with Grecian scenery that appears in stanzas xix. and xx. of the 'Hymn on the Nativity,' and also in the description of Athens in the *Paradise Regained*," familiarity acquired, of course, by study and poetic insight.

It is obvious, also, that the poetical use of the word Helicon did not proceed from ignorance of one of the tritest common-places of a time when poetry was much adorned with classical mythology, in a writer who directly afterwards enshrined a thought from Martial in verse that could have been written only by one greater than Martial. Milton delighted in this kind of adaptation, and the skill with which he assimilated to his own thought passages or phrases from the Greek and Latin poets is old matter of admiration among his editors and critics. From the very epigram of Martial which suggested the entombed bee in this epitaph, Milton drew the closing thought of his lines upon Shakespeare—"That kings for such a tomb would wish to die" (*Credibile est ipsam sic voluisse mori*). To say nothing of the adaptations from Homer and Virgil which abound in *Paradise Lost,*

I may mention Milton's literal translation of the description of Apollo's hair in the Argonautics of Apollonius Rhodius, which he transfers to Adam, in whom

> " Hyacinthine locks
> Round from his parted forelock manly hung
> Clustering ;"

the passage of Iphigenia in Tauris paraphrased in Comus's description of her brothers to the Lady; the passage in the Homeric Hymn to Apollo recalled by the lines in the 11th book of *Paradise Lost*, beginning

> " Then shall this mount
> Of Paradise by might of waves be moved
> Out of his place," &c.

Milton's poetry abounds in such recollections, and in touches from Ariosto or Tasso, which, in his day and before it, gave always additional pleasure to the educated reader by whom their source was recognized.

But some may say that all this is too true. The new poem is too like Milton's writing in its phraseology and turns of thought, and therefore somebody must have amused himself in piecing together an ingenious imitation. But does a coiner make his base money of gold? The poem is not only in Milton's manner, but it speaks his mind. Doubtless, it is a sketch wanting in some places the last touches of the master. Yet who but Milton could have left us such a sketch? Some of its imagery and outward beauty would have been attainable, as Mr. Goodhart has well observed, by Cowley at his best. But at the soul of it there is a grandeur as of Milton only. A mere imitator of Milton, with a mind capable of no higher aspiration than the chance of cheating somebody with a forged style, would hardly have advanced beyond the reproduction of old thoughts to a new effort to represent that mystery which is the subject of this Epitaph,—the resurrection of the dust

itself; the mystery of life in death; of the corruptible
that, in the great day to come, shall put on incorrup-
tion. This is the central thought of the Epitaph, fore-
shadowed in the first four lines, and expressed, as so
large and difficult a conception could only be expressed,
by labour of imagination in the close :—

> " He whom Heaven did call away
> Out of this hermitage of clay
> Has left some reliques in this urn,
> As a pledge of his return."

The pledge of resurrection in the buried ashes of the
dead, the subject of the poem, the thought which unites
it together, is thus shortly expressed in its opening
lines. Meanwhile, he lies here dead who sported with
the Muses, and the Muses mourn; but he being dead
yet lives, and with a fine poetical transition from the
customary strain of grief, which is confined to a dozen
lines, and expressed only that it may be so interrupted,
the voice rises from the grave. My grave, it says, be
it rich or poor, is nothing to me. A bee in amber is
enshrined more gloriously than the Pharaohs. Within
the grave my dust sleeps, curtained round. My nobler
part lies yet within your hearts, and here, in this dust
of the grave itself, is life. Life has not all passed from
these ashes. The seed of form is in this chaos of the
corrupted body; the thread of life is untwisted; ex-
istence is returned to its first principles; nature lies
cradled here, as in its infancy. This plant (and a plant,
it will be remembered, is so called from being set in the
ground, while the word suggests immediately the process
of nature most nearly resembling resurrection from
the dust)—this plant, thus calcined into dust, must rest
in its ashes until the returning soul breathe into it a
softening prolific fire. Then it shall spring forth and

renew its blossom. The chill of death shall yield to a diviner heat than human wisdom comprehends.

The suggestion of revival from the dust with which the poem closes, is directly taken from the old doctrine of Palingenesis, by which, says Isaac Disraeli, in his chapter on "Dreams at the Dawn of Philosophy," "Schott, Kircher, Gaffarel, Borelli, Digby, and the whole of that admirable school, discovered in the ashes of plants their primitive forms, which were again raised up by the force of heat . . . The process of Palingenesis, this picture of immortality, is described. These philosophers, having burnt a flower, by calcination disengaged the salts from its ashes, and deposited them in a glass phial; a chemical mixture acted on it . . . This dust thus excited by heat shoots upward into its primitive forms." As the heat passes away the form fades. Hence the allusion to the "more than chymick heat," that shall produce the last great Palingenesis of man. As to the other imagery, Psyche, it may be observed, is used, as here, and even with Cupid and Adonis, in the purely religious close to *Comus*, spoken by the Attendant Spirit.

One question remains unanswered that must have occurred to many readers of this poem. Whose death suggested it? In October, 1647, William Cartwright, who was not unworthy of an epitaph from Milton, had been dead nearly four years; but the collection of his comedies and other verse, to which some 50 of the wits and poets of the day prefixed memorial lines, was not published until 1651. One has only to observe how immeasurably the new Epitaph overtops the work of all the 50 to form some notion of its author's place among the writers of his time. It is possible that, although Milton, under the Commonwealth, would not join his

verse to that of Royalist wits before a volume of comedies, he too had found a theme in the early death of
the young man of genius who was at once wit, poet,
philosopher, and divine. About two years before the
date of this Epitaph died also William Habington, the
author of the purest love poetry written in the time of
Charles I.; and, although Habington was a Catholic,
Milton would have appreciated that character in the
author of *Castara*.

I know no other poets, newly dead, upon whom these
lines could have been written; but I do know of a
musician, dearly loved by Milton, then only a few months
in the grave, to whom he addressed the most beautiful
of the Latin poems in the volume to which this Epitaph
is added,—his own father. The elder Milton, scrivener
though he had been, ranked with the good musicians of
his time. Pieces of his composing are in two contemporary collections of sacred music. To this day his
arrangements of the psalm tunes "Norwich" and
"York" are in use; and Professor Masson, in his very
valuable first part of the *Life of Milton*, quotes a statement of Sir John Hawkins as to the tenor part of
"York tune," that "within memory half the nurses in
England were used to sing it by way of lullaby." The
poet's father died, says Professor Masson, in March,
1646-7; and Aubrey states that he read without spectacles at eighty-four. But if this Epitaph was—as it
may possibly have been—a thought of immortality over
his father's grave, Milton would have remembered the
dead not as he was only at the end of life, but as he had
known him during all the years of his own growth; as
he knew him when, tenderly expostulating with his
Puritanic prejudices against verse-writing, he pointed to
his father's own delight in music and said—I quote

Cowper's translation of the Latin verses—while styling him "heir by right indisputable of Arion's fame,"—

> "Thou hast thy gift, and I
> Mine also, and between us we receive,
> Father and Son, the whole inspiring God."

Professor Brewer and Professor Masson are of opinion that Milton had no leisure for writing verse in 1647. "From 1645 until the total loss of his sight," says Mr. Brewer, "the poet was engaged upon his Treatises on Divorce, the Tenure of Kings and Magistrates, written in his sternest mood, on his Defence of the People of England, and in his duties as Latin secretary." The reply to this is clear. The Doctrine of Divorce, the Judgment of Martin Bucer, Tetrachordon, and Colasterion, all appeared in or before the year 1645, in which Milton found time to arrange his poems for the press. He published little or nothing in the years 1646-7-8. The Tenure of Kings and Magistrates was written after the sentence on the king, which, in 1647, was not at all in question. Milton was not Latin secretary to the Commonwealth before the Commonwealth existed, and his reply to Salmasius did not occupy his mind before the production of the work, even before the occasion of the work, that he replied to. "Three years," says a biographer of Milton, "elapsed without any new publications from his pen, a silence which the various affecting occurrences in his family would naturally produce." To the middle of this period of three years belongs the poem now under discussion. At this time he was living, says his nephew, in great privacy, and perpetually engaged in a variety of studies. Professor Masson writes that "about the year 1647, Milton was engaged, as far as I have heard, in more thunderous work than the pursuit of bees, or the study

d

of honey-making." It is nowhere said that he chased bees or learnt to make honey, but I doubt whether any man's work can be so thunderous, least of all Milton's, as to leave him no time for a thought of immortality, and that, too, in the year of his father's death.

The last stand made against Milton's authorship of the new Poem has been on the recurrence in it of the word "its." I shall not take advantage of the mistake made by one objector, who asserts that this word occurs only three times in Shakespeare, or be content simply to show Lord Winchilsea's error in believing that the word "its" was not used by Milton. The true difficulty, which I have not seen fully stated, would be incompletely met by arguments which would dispose of such objections. In brief, these are the facts. The neuter genitive originally corresponded to the masculine; the declension being he, she, it ; his, her, his. Originally also, there was a complex distribution of genders among things animate and inanimate, as there is now in German. As inflexions disappeared and grammatical forms were simplified, we arrived at a very convenient solution of the difficulty with the genders. Apart from figurative speech, and with a few logical exceptions, as in the word child, every male creature was masculine, every female feminine, and all that was not actually he or she was neuter. Then gradually there began to be felt some need of an occasional distinction between masculine and neuter in the inflected cases of the demonstrative pronoun. "It" stood for "him" in the dative, sometimes also in the genitive, as in Ben Jonson's *Silent Woman* (Act II., sc. 3), "*It* knighthood and *it* friends," and in *King Lear*, " You know, nuncle, the hedge sparrow fed the cuckoo so long that it's (it has) had *it* head bit off by *it* young." " It," as a neuter genitive, is thus used at

he present day in some of our north-western counties.
But in the construction of good English "it" served
badly for a genitive, and at the end of the reign of
Elizabeth the form "its" was beginning to come into
use. In the reign of James I. this form was slowly
making way. The authorised translation of the Bible,
based upon an elder version, is almost[1] without it, and
the best writers seldom used it without a distinct reason
for doing so. Thus, in *Measure for Measure*, " Heaven
grant us *its* peace, but not the King of Hungary's," was
a form of avoiding what might look like an irreverent
antithesis between the persons of God and the King of
Hungary. Yet here is a passage from the *Winter's
Tale* (Act I., sc. 2) printed before the accession of
Charles I. in which the word "its," most rare as it
usually is in Shakespeare, occurs three times in seven
lines, and that, too, where need for it is not strong.

> " How sometimes Nature will betray *its* folly,
> *Its* tenderness, and make itself a pastime
> To harder bosoms! Looking on the lines
> Of my boy's face, methought I did recoil
> Twenty-three years, and saw myself unbreeched,
> In my green velvet coat, my dagger muzzled
> Lest it should bite *its* master."

In the reign of Charles I. the use of "its," established
by the need of such a word, became much more familiar. George Herbert, dead before 1647, wrote—

> " Sweet rose, whose hue angry and brave
> Bids the rash gazer wipe his eye,
> Thy root is ever in *its* grave,
>   And thou must die."

Lovelace wrote for the curtain of Lucasta's picture—

---

[1] " Its " occurs in Levit. xxv. 5; and perhaps elsewhere.

> "—Her fair soul's in all
> So truly copied from the originall,
> That you will swear her body by this law
> Is but *its* shadow, as this *its*—now draw."

Cowley wrote—

> "What pity in my breast does reign,
> Methinks I feel, too, all *its* pain."

The word, in fact, had in 1647 become common. But the true argument is—and I have no wish to evade it—that, common as the use of the word had become, Milton followed the elder poets, was a master of the language, and avoided indiscriminate use of the modern form. Nearly twenty years before the date of the Epitaph, Milton, in the *Hymn on the Nativity*, wrote of Nature that she—

> "Now was almost won
> To think her part was done,
> And that her reign had here *its* last fulfilling."

Put "his" for "its," and the reason for the adoption of the new form becomes obvious. The equivocal "his" was to be avoided in a context which included double use of the word "her." So in *Paradise Lost* (Book I. l. 254)—

> "The mind is *its* own place, and in itself
> Can make a heaven of hell, a hell of heaven;"

the necessary use of the word "itself" made the use of "its" preferable to "his" in association with it. Or take the famous lines (Book IV., l. 810-14):—

> "Him thus intent Ithuriel with his spear
> Touch'd lightly; for no falsehood can endure
> Touch of celestial temper, but returns
> Of force to *its* own likeness: up he starts
> Discovered and surprised."

Had "his" been used for "its," the equivocal gender would have connected itself inconveniently with the " he" which follows.

Now, although a looser use of "its" might have been permitted for once to Milton in a piece not polished for the Press—since we find the word used loosely three times in seven lines of a finished work of Shakespeare, who wrote when the employment of it was far more exceptional—I enter no such plea. Let us rather see whether Milton's own test will not bear strict application to the occurrences of the word "its" in the Epitaph.

> "With whom *he* sported ere the day
>   Budded forth *its* tender ray—"

is precisely one of the cases in which Milton would avoid the equivocal genitive. Substitute " his " for " its," and the reason becomes obvious. The other three occurrences of " its" are virtually one, since they are all part of the same construction. The repetition of "his" would have injured the poetry by not excluding a suggestion of masculine remains which the feminine Psyche shall " in *her* fostering arms enfold." To the very essence of the thought belonged reduction of man's body to an " it," which yet contains the germ of life, and absolute shutting out of all suggestion of a sexual relation in the return of the soul to the body that springs up again out of its dust.

There remains only the question of handwriting. If the poem be in Milton's autograph, his authorship becomes indisputable. If not, this piece is in the position of other poems written before his blindness, which come down to us in a handwriting either not his, or supposed to be that of a copyist. Milton's natural and unrestricted handwriting was large and bold, but, he was skilful with the pen, and when restricted by space to a cramped form, or in the act of copying, would fall into such variations of style as we know, in our own experience, to be usual to a practised hand.

In Milton's case this difficulty is complicated by the facts, that often before his blindness, and always after it, he used an amanuensis, and that the quantity of his undoubted handwriting, now left to us, is not large. In the British Museum there is very little. The most precious collection is that kept in a glass-case at Trinity College, Cambridge, a volume of original MSS. of Milton's earlier period, including drafts, with his corrections, of Comus and Lycidas. The facsimile now published of the MS. of the Epitaph will enable those who have ready access to this collection, or more especially to examples of Milton's small hand upon margins or fly leaves of books, to make, with the requisite thoroughness, the direct comparison on which alone, a safe opinion can be based. That the scrutiny may take the right direction, I add here a letter addressed to the *Times*, in which Mr. Bond, the experienced Keeper of the MSS. in the British Museum, defines the ground of his belief that it is not the handwriting of Milton :—

" Sir,—As my opinion on the handwriting and signature of the poem ascribed to Milton has been referred to by writers in the controversy, I think it becoming to state it publicly and in my own words.

" I have several times examined both writing and signature, and always with the same conclusion, that the writing is not Milton's, and the signature is not ' J. M.'

" The difference between Milton's handwriting and that of the poem is perceptible in their general character ; and it is important to study the expression

in discriminating handwritings. The firm and some-
what rigid characters of Milton are not in harmony with
the light, pliant, and rather weak forms of the poem.

"Applying the test of comparison of particular letters,
I find essential variations in the two writings. Characteristic forms used by Milton are not found in the
writing of the poem.

"It has been pleaded that some letters are found
similarly formed in the two writings. But on such
grounds volumes of anonymous verses might be fathered
on Milton. The differences in forms of letters are too
considerable in the present case to be disregarded.

"Some of these differences have been questioned on
the authority of certain pieces included in Sotheby's
specimens, which are themselves of doubtful genuineness.
One of these, the verses found in the *Mel Heliconium*,
Mr. Masson has recently condemned; and I also remember to have examined it and declared it not of Milton's
writing many years ago.

"In addition to the evidence of general expression
and the forms of letters, I would refer to the ortho-
graphy and the contractions of words used in the poem.
Both forms of spelling and contractions I find foreign
to Milton's common use in the year 1647.[1] Indeed, there
is ground for surmising that the poem is by the hand of
a copyist. The word "nature" in the twelfth line from

---

[1] This argument founded upon spelling is much open to question. It is in no man's power to define precisely how Milton
would have spelt a word in a particular year of his life. Except
in the case of a few words, Milton's spelling varied like that of
his neighbours. I have before me an exact copy, made in
1792, of Milton's MSS. in Trinity College, and find by comparison of spelling my belief that Milton was here the copyist
of his own lines distinctly strengthened.

the end is written with a stroke of contraction over the a, and without the t. This is not a true contraction, and would not have been used by the author in writing his lines. The poem has probably been transcribed from a draught copy, and the word written down as imperfectly deciphered by the scribe.

"The more important question, as determining authorship, is as to the signature. I have closely examined it, both with the naked eye and under strong magnifying power, and have always come to the same conclusion. The first of the two letters is a ' P,' similar in form to that used in the word 'Psyche' in the poem itself. The second is an unquestioned 'M,' but not of the form used by Milton.

"British Museum, July 25. "EDW. A. BOND."

It is fair also to point attention to the difference of opinion among experts indicated by the fact that the editor of the *Athenæum* records in his journal that he examined the signature to the MS. Epitaph "in a good light, with two magnifying glasses, in the presence of four officers of the British Museum. We all resolved the signature into J. M." As the object of this controversy, happily so free from bitterness, is not to prevail in combat, but to ascertain truth, I reply to the denial that the handwriting as well as the poetry of the Epitaph is Milton's, by publishing a facsimile as the best help to a true settlement of that part of the question.

One or two suggestions, however, bearing upon this part of the argument I wish to add. That there are obvious affinities between the writing of a little off-hand complimentary inscription in a book called the *Mel Heliconium*, and the writing of this Epitaph. That Mr. Bond long since denied that inscription to be in

Milton's writing upon grounds which were not unsuccessfully disputed, and were not held to be satisfactory by the late Mr. Sotheby in the volume which contains the result of his special research into the handwriting of Milton; Mr. Sotheby being hitherto the only man who has made the difficult subject of Milton's handwriting a special study. That the probabilities are very great indeed against the writing by any one else than Milton of a thoroughly Miltonic piece at the back of a printed leaf of Milton's first collection of his poems; this being done only two years after its first publication, before Milton's name had become a power. The improbability is enormously increased by the fact that this unknown second Milton must have had a name beginning with M. and a Christian name of which the initial, when faded and half obliterated, as it now is, bears, at least, a strong resemblance to a J. It is to be observed, too, that the denial of this letter to be a J, and declaration upon doubtful evidence of one small scratch that it must be a P, sets out from the presumption of a uniformity and freedom from occasional chance touches of the pen, which is not to be found in the known signatures of Milton, and is rare in the signature of any man. It is also not unworthy of notice that Mr. Bond finds in the line " A vitall tincture still retain," the word "still" to have been written over the word "yet." This is a change more likely to have been made by an author copying his own lines than by a mere transcriber. And whoever may be the transcriber of this Epitaph, the author of it is John Milton.

August 4, 1868.   H. M.

CONTENTS.

PART 1.

WITH THE KING.

l

CONTENTS.

PART II.

WITH THE COMMONS.

An Epitaph.

Whom Heaven did call away
Out of this Hermitage of clay,
And left some reliques on thy Urne
A pledge of his returne.
And all the Muses doe deplore
The losse of this their paramour
With whom he sported every day
And led forth his kinder ray.
And now Apollo hands his layes
And puts on Cypres for his bayes.
The sacred Sisters tune their quills
And to ye blubbering rills
And as still of his doome they thinke upon
And make their owne teares their Helicon
Having the two-topt mount divine
The votaries to his shrine.
Thinke not (reader) mee lesse blest
Sleeping in this narrow chest
Then if my ashes did lie hid
Under some stately pyramid.
A rich tombe make happy, the
That liveth, was happier farr then mee
That lie buried in the thymie wood
And freshed by the golden flood,
And from the Amber-weeping Tree
With which downe so plenteously.
And so this little wanton life
Most gloriously girds it selfe.
A tombe whose beauty might compare
With Cleopatras sepulcher.
In this little bed my dust
Ingraved round I here entrust,

CAVALIER AND PURITAN SONG.

Part I.

WITH THE KING.

I'll love good wine,
I'll love my book and Muse,
Nay, all the Nine;
I'll love my real friend,
I'll love my horse; and could I choose
One that would not my love abuse,
To her my heart should bend.
I will love those that laugh, and those that sing,
I'll love my country, prince and laws, and those that love my King.

ALEXANDER BROME.

LUCASTA. GOING TO THE WARS.

ELL me not, sweet, I am unkind,
  That from the nunnery
Of thy chaste breast and quiet mind
  To war and arms I fly;

True, a new mistress now I chase,
  The first foe in the field;
And, with a stronger faith embrace
  A sword, a horse, a shield.

Yet this inconstancy is such
  As you too shall adore;
I could not love you, dear, so much,
  Loved I not honour more.

Richard Lovelace.

THE DIFFERENCE BETWIXT KINGS AND SUBJECTS.

WIXT kings and subjects there's this mighty odds,
  Subjects are taught by men; kings by the gods.

Robert Herrick.

IN THE WOODS.

THRICE happy he who by some shady grove,
　　Far from the clamorous world, doth live his own,
　　Though solitary, who is not alone,
But doth converse with that eternal love.
O how more sweet is bird's harmonious moan,
Or the hoarse sobbings of the widow'd dove,
Than those smooth whisp'rings near a prince's throne,
Which good make doubtful, do the evil approve!
O how more sweet is zephyrs' wholesome breath,
And sighs embalm'd which new-born flow'rs unfold,
Than that applause vain honour doth bequeath!
How sweet are streams to poison drank in gold!
　The world is full of horrors, troubles, slights:
　Woods' harmless shades have only true delights.

William Drummond.

A DIRGE.

GLORIES, pleasures, pomps, delights and ease,
　　Can but please
　　The outward senses, when the mind
Is or untroubled, or by peace refined.
Crowns may flourish and decay,
Beauties shine, but fade away.
Youth may revel, yet it must
Lie down in a bed of dust.
Earthly honours flow and waste,
Time alone doth change and last.
Sorrows mingled with contents, prepare
　　Rest for care;
Love only reigns in death; though art
Can find no comfort for a broken heart.

John Ford.

DEATH'S FINAL CONQUEST.

THE glories of our birth and state
　　Are shadows, not substantial things;
　There is no armour against fate;
Death lays his icy hands on kings.
　　　Sceptre and crown
　　　Must tumble down,
And in the dust be equal made
With the poor crooked scythe and spade.

Some men with swords may reap the field,
　And plant fresh laurels where they kill;
But their strong nerves at last must yield;
　They tame but one another still.
　　　Early or late,
　　　They stoop to fate,
And must give up their murmuring breath,
When they, pale captives, creep to death.

The garlands wither on your brow,
　Then boast no more your mighty deeds;
Upon death's purple altar now,
　See where the victor victim bleeds.
　　　All heads must come
　　　To the cold tomb;
Only the actions of the just
Smell sweet and blossom in the dust.

James Shirley.

CONSTANCY.

UT upon it. I have loved
  Three whole days together;
And am like to love three more,
If it prove fair weather.

Time shall moult away his wings
  Ere he shall discover
In the whole wide world again
  Such a constant lover.

But the spite on't is, no praise
  Is due at all to me:
Love with me had made no stays,
  Had it any been but she.

Had it any been but she
  And that very face,
There had been at least ere this
  A dozen dozen in her place.

Sir John Suckling.

HY dost thou say I am forsworn,
  Since thine I vow'd to be?
Lady, it is already morn;
  It was last night I swore to thee
  That fond impossibility.

Yet have I loved thee well, and long;
  A tedious twelve-hours' space!
I should all other beauties wrong,
  And rob thee of a new embrace,
  Did I still dote upon that face.   [3 *st.*

Richard Lovelace.

THE EPICURE.

FILL the bowl with rosy wine,
    Around our temples roses twine,
    And let us cheerfully awhile
Like the wine and roses smile.
Crown'd with roses we contemn
Gyges' wealthy diadem.
To-day is ours, what do we fear?
To-day is ours, we have it here.
Let's treat it kindly, that it may
Wish at least with us to stay.
Let's banish business, banish sorrow,
To the gods belongs to-morrow.

                     Abraham Cowley.

A SONG OF SACK.

COME let us drink away the time,   [1 *l.*
    When wine runs high, wit's in the prime,
    Drink and stout drinkers are true joys;
Odd sonnets, and such little toys
Are exercises fit for boys.

The whining lover that doth place
His fancy on a painted face,
And wastes his substance in the chase,
Would ne'er in melancholy pine
Had he affections so divine
As once to fall in love with wine.

Then to our liquor let us sit;
Wine makes the soul for action fit.
Who drinks most wine hath the most wit:

The gods themselves do revels keep,
And in pure nectar tipple deep
When slothful mortals are asleep:

The gods then let us imitate,
Secure from carping care and fate;
Wine, wit and courage both create.
In wine Apollo always chose
His darkest oracles to disclose,
'Twas wine gave him his ruby-nose.

Who dares not drink's a wretched wight,
Nor do I think that man dares fight
All day, that dares not drink at night:
Come fill my cup until it swim
With foam, that overlooks the brim.
Who drinks the deepest? Here's to him.

Sobriety and Study breeds
Suspicion in our acts and deeds;
The downright drunkard no man heeds.
Give me but sack, tobacco store,
A drunken friend—I'll ask no more.   [1 *l.*

John Cleveland.

THE RAINBOW.

LOOK how the rainbow doth appear
But in one only hemisphere;
So likewise after our decease,
No more is seen the arch of peace.
That cov'nant's here, the under-bow,
That nothing shoots but war and woe.

Robert Herrick.

THE SHADOW.

LIFE a right shadow is ;
   For if it long appear,
   Then is it spent, and death's long night draws
        near ;
Shadows are moving, light,
And is there aught so moving as is this ?
When it is most in sight
It steals away, and none knows how or where,
So near our cradles to our coffins are.

                   William Drummond.

ANACREONTIC.

INVEST my head with fragrant rose,
   That on fair Flora's bosom grows !
   Distend my veins with purple juice,
That mirth may through my soul diffuse.
   'Tis wine and love, and love in wine
   Inspires our youth with flames divine.

Thus, crown'd with Paphian myrtle, I
In Cyprian shades will bathing lie ;
Whose snows if too much cooling, then
Bacchus shall warm my blood again.
     'Tis wine and love, and love in wine
     Inspires our youth with flames divine.

Life's short and winged pleasures fly ;
Who mourning live, do living die.

On down and floods then, swan-like, I
Will stretch my limbs, and singing die.
    'Tis wine and love, and love in wine,
    Inspires our youth with flames divine.
                      Robert Heath.

UNGRATEFUL BEAUTY THREATENED.

KNOW Celia, (since thou art so proud,)
    'Twas I that gave thee thy renown ;
    Thou hadst, in the forgotten crowd
Of common beauties, lived unknown,
Had not my verse exhaled thy name,
And with it impt the wings of fame.

That killing power is none of thine,
    I gave it to thy voice and eyes ;
Thy sweets, thy graces, all are mine ;
    Thou art my star, shin'st in my skies :
Then dart not from thy borrow'd sphere
Lightning on him that fix'd thee there.

Tempt me with such affrights no more,
    Lest what I made I uncreate,
Let fools thy mystic forms adore,
    I'll know thee in thy mortal state :.
Wise poets, that wrapt truth in tales,
Knew her themselves through all her veils.
                      Thomas Carew.

DRINKING SONG.

COME, let the state stay
And drink away,
There is no business above it:
It warms the cold brain,
Makes us speak in high strain,
He's a fool that does not approve it.
The Macedon youth
Left behind him this truth,
That nothing is done with much thinking;
He drunk and he fought,
Till he had what he sought:
The world was his own by good drinking.

Sir John Suckling.

YOUNG FOLLY.

FINE young Folly, tho' you were
That fair beauty I did swear,
Yet you ne'er could reach my heart;
For we courtiers learn at school,
Only with your sex to fool—
You're not worth the serious part.

When I sigh and kiss your hand,
Cross my arms, and wond'ring stand,
Holding parley with your eye:
Then dilate on my desires,
Swear the sun ne'er shot such fires,
All is but a handsome lie.

When I eye your curl or lace,
Gentle soul, you think your face
    Straight some murder doth commit;
And your virtue doth begin
To grow scrupulous of my sin,
    When I talk to show my wit.

Therefore, madam, wear no cloud,
Nor to check my love grow proud,
    For in sooth, I much do doubt
'Tis the powder on your hair,
Not your breath, perfumes the air,
    And your clothes that set you out.

Yet though truth has this confess'd,
And I vow I love in jest,
    When I next begin to court,
And protest an amorous flame,
You will swear I in earnest am,
    Bedlam! this is pretty sport.
                              William Habington.

THE SURPRISE.

HERE'S no dallying with love,
    Though he be a child and blind;
    Then let none the danger prove,
    Who would to himself be kind;
Smile he does when thou dost play,
But his smiles to death betray.

Lately with the boy I sported,
    Love I did not, yet love feign'd;
Had not mistress, yet I courted;
    Sigh I did, yet was not pain'd;

'Till at last this love in jest
Proved in earnest my unrest.

When I saw my fair one first,
    In a feigned fire I burn'd;
But true flames my poor heart pierced
    When her eyes on mine she turn'd:
So a real wound I took
For my counterfeited look.   [2 *st.*

None who loves not then make shew,
    Love's as ill deceived as fate;
Fly the boy, he'll cog and woo;
    Mock him, and he wounds thee straight.
Ah! who dally boast in vain;
False love wants not real pain.

                                   Edward Sherburne.

GOOD COUNSEL TO A YOUNG MAID.

WHEN you the sun-burnt pilgrim see,
        Fainting with thirst, haste to the springs;
    Mark how, at first with bended knee
        He courts the crystal nymphs, and flings
His body to the earth, where he
Prostrate adores the flowing deity.

But when this sweaty face is drench'd
    In her cool waves, when from her sweet
Bosom his burning thirst is quench'd;
    Then mark how with disdainful feet
He kicks her banks, and from the place,
That thus refresh'd him, moves with sullen pace.

So shalt thou be despised, fair maid,
  When by the sated lover tasted ;
What first he did with tears invade,
  Shall afterwards with scorn be wasted :
When all thy virgin-springs grow dry,
When no streams shall be left, but in thine eye.

                          Thomas Carew.

TO CASTARA.

IVE me a heart where no impure
    Disorder'd passions rage ;
   Which jealousy doth not obscure,
  Nor vanity t' expense engage ;
Nor woo'd to madness by quaint oaths,
Or the fine rhetoric of clothes,
  Which not the softness of the age
To vice or folly doth decline :
Give me that heart, Castara, for 'tis thine.

Take thou a heart, where no new look
  Provokes new appetite :
With no fresh charm of beauty took,
  Or wanton stratagem of wit ;
Not idly wandering here and there,
Led by an amorous eye or ear ;
  Aiming each beauteous mark to hit ;
Which virtue doth to one confine :
Take thou that heart, Castara, for 'tis mine. [1 *st.*

                        William Habington.

CONSTANCY.

WHO is the honest man?
    He that doth still and strongly good pursue,
    To God, his neighbour, and himself most true:
            Whom neither force nor fawning can
Unpin, or wrench from giving all their due.

            Whose honesty is not
So loose or easy, that a ruffling wind
Can blow away, or glittering look it blind:
            Who rides his sure and even trot,
While the world now rides by, now lags behind.

            Who, when great trials come,
Nor seeks, nor shuns them; but doth calmly stay,
Till he the thing and the example weigh:
            All being brought into a sum,
What place or person calls for, he doth pay.

            Whom none can work or woo,
To use in any thing a trick or sleight;
For above all things he abhors deceit:
            His words and works and fashion too
All of a piece, and all are clear and straight.

            Who never melts or thaws
At close temptations: when the day is done,
His goodness sets not, but in dark can run:
            The sun to others writeth laws,
And is their virtue; virtue is his sun.

            Who, when he is to treat
With sick folks, women, those whom passions sway,
Allows for that, and keeps his constant way:
            Whom others' faults do not defeat;
But though men fail him, yet his part doth play.

Whom nothing can procure,
When the wild world runs bias, from his will
To writhe his limbs, and share, not mend the ill.
This is the marksman, safe and sure,
Who still is right, and prays to be so still.

George Herbert.

LOVING AND BELOVED.

HERE never yet was honest man
　　That ever drove the trade of love;
It is impossible, nor can
Integrity our ends promove:
For kings and lovers are alike in this,
That their chief art in reign dissembling is.

Here we are loved, and there we love,
　　Good nature now and passion strive
Which of the two should be above,
　　And laws unto the other give.
So we false fire with art sometimes discover,
And the true fire with the same art do cover.

What rack can fancy find so high?
　　Here we must court, and here engage,
Though in the other place we die.
　　Oh! 'tis torture all, and cozenage;
And which the harder is I cannot tell,
To hide true love, or make false love look well.

Since it is thus, God of desire,
　　Give me my honesty again,
And take thy brands back, and thy fire:
　　I am weary of the state I am in.
Since (if the very best should not befall)
Love's triumph must be Honour's funeral.

Sir John Suckling.

TO THE KING.

IVE way, give way ; now, now my Charles shines
   here,
  A public light, in this immensive sphere ;
Some stars were fix'd before, but these are dim,
Compared, in this my ample orb, to him.
Draw in your feeble fires, while that he
Appears but in his meaner majesty ;
Where, if such glory flashes from his name,
Which is his shade, who can abide his flame !
Princes, and such-like public lights as these,
Must not be look'd on but at distances ;
For, if we gaze on these brave lamps too near,
Our eyes they 'll blind, or if not blind, they 'll bleer.
       Robert Herrick.

TO THE QUEEN.

[10 *ll.*

N whom th' extremes of power and beauty move,
  The Queen of Britain and the Queen of Love.
   As the bright sun (to which we owe no sight
Of equal glory to your beauty's light)
Is wisely placed in so sublime a seat,
T' extend his light, and moderate his heat :
So happy 'tis you move in such a sphere
As your high majesty with awful fear
In human breasts might qualify that fire,
Which, kindled by those eyes, had flamed higher
Than when the scorched world like hazard run,
By the approach of the ill-guided sun.
No other nymphs have title to men's hearts,
But as their meanness larger hope imparts :

    c

Your beauty more the fondest lover moves
With admiration than his private loves ;
With admiration ! for a pitch so high
(Save sacred Charles his) never Love durst fly.
Heaven that preferr'd a sceptre to your hand,
Favour'd our freedom more than your command :
Beauty had crown'd you, and you must have been
The whole world's mistress, other than a queen.
All had been rivals, and you might have spared,
Or kill'd and tyrannized without a guard.
No power achieved, either by arms or birth,
Equals Love's empire, both in heaven and earth.
Such eyes as yours on Jove himself have thrown
As bright and fierce a lightning as his own :
Witness our Jove, prevented by their flame
In his swift passage to th' Hesperian dame ;
When, like a lion, finding in his way
To some intended spoil a fairer prey,
The royal youth pursuing the report
Of beauty, found it in the Gallic court ;
There public care with private passion fought
A doubtful combat in his noble thought :
Should he confess his greatness and his love,
And the free faith of your great brother prove,
With his Achates breaking through the cloud
Of that disguise which did their graces shroud,
And, mixing with those gallants at the ball,
Dance with the ladies and outshine them all ;
Or on his journey o'er the mountains ride ?
So when the fair Leucothoe he spied,
To check his steeds impatient Phœbus yearn'd,
Though all the world was in his course concern'd.
What may hereafter her meridian do,
Whose dawning beauty warm'd his bosom so ? [4 *ll.*
                                    Edmund Waller.

THE PURITAN.

WITH face and fashion to be known
　　For one of sure election,
　With eyes all white, and many a groan,
With neck aside to draw in tone,
With harp in 's nose, or he is none:
　　See a new teacher of the town,
　　O the town, O the town's new teacher!

With pate cut shorter than the brow,
With little ruff starch'd you know how,
With cloak like Paul, no cape I trow;
With surplice none; but lately now.
With hands to thump, no knees to bow.
　　See a new teacher of the town,
　　O the town, O the town's new teacher!

With coz'ning cough and hollow cheek,
To get new gatherings every week,
With paltry change of *and* to *eke*,
With some small Hebrew, and no Greek,
To find out words where stuff's to seek.
　　See a new teacher of the town,
　　O the town, O the town's new teacher!

With shop-board breeding and intrusion,
With some outlandish institution,
With Ursin's catechism to muse on,
With System's method for confusion,
With grounds strong laid of mere illusion.
　　See a new teacher of the town,
　　O the town, O the town's new teacher!

With rites indifferent all damnèd,
And made unlawful, if commanded,

Good works of Popery down banded,
And moral laws from him estranged,
Except the Sabbath still unchanged.
    See a new teacher of the town,
      O the town, O the town's new teacher!

With speech unthought, quick revelation,
With boldness in predestination,
With threats of absolute damnation,
For *yea* and *nay* hath some salvation
For his own tribe, not every nation.
    See a new teacher of the town,
      O the town, O the town's new teacher!

With after-licence cost a crown,
When bishop new had put him down,
With tricks call'd repetition,
And doctrine newly brought to town,
Of teaching men to hang and drown.
    See a new teacher of the town,
      O the town, O the town's new teacher!

With flesh provision to keep Lent,
With shelves of sweetmeats often spent,
Which new maid bought, old lady sent,
Though to be saved a poor present;
Yet legacies assure the event.
    See a new teacher of the town,
      O the town, O the town's new teacher!

With troops expecting him at th' door,
That would hear sermons, and no more;
With noting tools, and sighs great store,
With Bibles great to turn them o'er,
While he wrests places by the score.
    See a new teacher of the town,
      O the town, O the town's new teacher!

With running text, the nam'd forsaken,
With *for* and *but*, both by sense shaken,
Cheap doctrines forced, wild uses taken,
Both sometimes one, by mark mistaken,
With anything to any shapen.
   See a new teacher of the town,
     O the town, O the town's new teacher!

With new-wrought caps, against the canon,
For taking cold, though sure he have none;
A sermon's end, where he began one—
A new hour long, when's glass had run one,
New use, new points, new notes to stand on.
   See a new teacher of the town,
     O the town, O the town's new teacher!
               John Cleveland.

UPON THE TROUBLESOME TIMES.

! Times most bad,
    Without the scope
       Of hope
Of better to be had!

   Where shall I go,
    Or whither run
      To shun
This public overthrow?

   No places are,
    This I am sure,
      Secure
In this our wasting war.

   Some storms we have past;
    Yet we must all
      Down fall,
And perish at the last.   *Robert Herrick.*

CHERRY RIPE.

CHERRY-RIPE, ripe, ripe, I cry,
    Full and fair ones; come, and buy:
    If so be you ask me where
They do grow? I answer, there,
Where my Julia's lips do smile,
There's the land, or cherry-isle!
Whose plantations fully show
All the year where cherries grow.

Robert Herrick.

LEUCASIA'S LULLABY.

SEAL up her eyes, O Sleep, but flow
    Mild as her manners to and fro:
    Slide softly into her that she
May receive no wound from thee.
And ye, present her thoughts, O Dreams,
With hushing winds and purling streams,
Whiles hovering Silence sits without
Careful to keep disturbance out.
Thus seize her, Sleep, thus her again resign,
So what was Heaven's gift we'll reckon thine.

William Cartwright.

STAPHYLA'S LULLABY.

QUIET sleep, or I will make
    Erinnys whip thee with a snake,
    And cruel Rhadamanthus take
Thy body to the boiling lake,
Where fire and brimstone never slake.
Thy heart shall burn; thy head shall ache,
And every joint about thee quake.
And therefore dare not yet to wake.

Quiet sleep, or thou shalt see
The horrid hags of Tartary,
Whose tresses ugly serpents be ;
And Cerberus shall bark at thee,
And all the furies that are three,
The worst is call'd Tisiphone,
Shall lash thee to eternity.
And therefore sleep thou peacefully.

Thomas Randolph.

ON HIS MAJESTY'S RECEIVING THE NEWS OF THE DUKE OF BUCKINGHAM'S DEATH.*

SO earnest with thy God, can no new care,
No sense of danger interrupt thy prayer ?
The sacred wrestler, till a blessing given,
Quits not his hold, but halting conquers Heaven ;
Nor was the stream of thy devotion stopp'd
When from the body such a limb was lopp'd,
As to thy present state was no less maim ;
Though thy wise choice has since repair'd the same.
Bold Homer durst not so great virtue feign
In his best pattern ; of Patroclus slain
With such amazement as weak mothers use,
And frantic gesture, he receives the news :
Yet fell his darling by th' impartial chance
Of war, imposed by royal Hector's lance ;
Thine in full peace, and by a vulgar hand
Torn from thy bosom, left his high command.

The famous painter could allow no place
For private sorrow in a prince's face :

---

* Without visible emotion.

Yet, that his piece might not exceed belief,
He cast a veil upon supposèd grief.

'Twas want of such a precedent as this
Made the old heathens frame their gods amiss.
Their Phœbus should not act a fonder part
For their fair boy, than he did for his heart;
Nor blame for Hyacinthus' fate his own
That kept from him wish'd death, hadst thou been known.

He that with thine shall weigh good David's deeds,
Shall find his passion, not his love, exceeds.
He cursed the mountains where his brave friend died,
But let false Ziba with his heir divide:
Where thy immortal love to thy best friends,
Like that of heaven, upon their seed descends.
Such huge extremes inhabit thy great mind,
God-like unmoved, and yet like woman kind.   [4 *ll.*
Edmund Waller.

THE HUNT.

THIS world a hunting is,
        The prey, poor man; the Nimrod fierce is
            Death;
His speedy greyhounds are
Lust, Sickness, Envy, Care;
Strife that ne'er falls amiss,
With all those ills which haunt us while we breathe.
Now, if by chance we fly
Of these the eager chace,
Old age with stealing pace
Casts on his nets, and there we panting die.
William Drummond.

THE HOCK-CART, OR HARVEST HOME.

OME sons of summer, by whose toil
We are the lords of wine and oil ;
By whose tough labours and rough hands
We rip up first, then reap our lands.
Crown'd with the ears of corn, now come,
And, to the pipe, sing harvest home.
Come forth, my lord, and see the cart
Drest up with all the country art.
See, here a maukin, there a sheet,
As spotless pure as it is sweet ;
The horses, mares, and frisking fillies,
Clad all in linen white as lilies.
The harvest swains and wenches bound
For joy to see the hock-cart crown'd.
About the cart hear how the rout
Of rural youngling raise the shout,
Pressing before, some coming after,
Those with a shout, and these with laughter.
Some bless the cart, some kiss the sheaves,
Some prank them up with oaken leaves ;
Some cross the fill-horse, some with great
Devotion stroke the home-borne wheat ;
While other rustics, less intent
To prayers than to merriment,
Run after with their breeches rent.
Well, on, brave boys ! to your lord's hearth,
Glitt'ring with fire, where, for your mirth,
Ye shall see first the large and chief
Foundation of your feast, fat beef ;
With upper stories, mutton, veal,
And bacon, which makes full the meal,

With several dishes standing by,
As, here a custard, there a pie,
And here all-tempting frumenty.
And for to make the merry cheer,
If smirking wine be wanting here,
There's that which drowns all care, stout beer;
Which freely drink to your lord's health,
Then to the plough, the commonwealth,
Next to your flails, your fanes, your fats;
Then to the maids with wheaten hats;
To the rough sickle, and the crookt scythe,
Drink, frolic, boys, till all be blithe.
Feed and grow fat, and as ye eat
Be mindful that the lab'ring neat,
As you, may have their full of meat;
And know, besides, ye must revoke
The patient ox unto the yoke,
And all go back unto the plough
And harrow, though they're hang'd up now.
And, you must know, your lord's word's true,
Feed him ye must, whose food fills you.
And that this pleasure is like rain,
Not sent ye for to drown your pain,
But for to make it spring again.

Robert Herrick.

THE LONG VACATION IN LONDON.

NOW town-wit says to witty friend,
    " Transcribe apace all thou hast penned;
      For I in journey hold it fit
To cry thee up to country-wit."

Our mules are come! dissolve the club!
The word till term, is rub, O rub!

Now gamester poor, in cloak of stammel,
Mounted on steed as slow as camel
Batoon of crab in luckless hand,
(Which serves for bilbo and for wand)
Early in morn does sneak from town
Lest landlord's wife should seize on crown;
On crown which he in pouch does keep,
When day is done to pay for sleep;
For he in journey nought does eat.
Host spies him come, cries, "Sir, what meat?"
He calls for room, and down he lies.
Quoth host, "No supper, sir?" He cries,
"I eat no supper, fling on rug!
I'm sick, d'you hear; yet, bring a jug!"

Now damsel young that dwells in Cheap
For very joy begins to leap;
Her elbow small she oft does rub,
Tickled with hope of sillabub!
For mother (who does gold maintain
On thumb, and keys in silver chain)
In snow-white clout wrapt nook of pie,
Fat capon's wing, and rabbit's thigh,
And said to hackney coachman, "Go.
Take shillings six, say ay or no."
"Whither?" says he. Quoth she, "Thy team
Shall drive to place where groweth cream."

But husband gray now comes to stall,
For prentice notch'd he straight does call:
"Where's dame?" quoth he. Quoth son of shop,
"She's gone her cake in milk to sop."

"Ho, ho! to Islington; enough!
Fetch Job my son, and our dog Ruff!
For there in pond, through mire and muck,
We'll cry, hey duck! there Ruff, hey duck!" [12 *ll.*

Now man that trusts, with weary thighs,
Seeks garret where small poet lies.
He comes to lane, finds garret shut;
Then not with knuckle, but with foot
He rudely thrusts, would enter doors;
Though poet sleeps not, yet he snores:
Cit chafes like beast of Lybia then,
Swears he'll not come or send again.
From little lump triangular
Poor poet's sighs are heard afar.
Quoth he, "Do noble numbers choose
To walk on feet that have no shoes?"
Then he does wish with fervent breath,
And as his last request ere death,
Each ode a bond, each madrigal
A lease from Haberdashers' Hall,
Or that he had protected been
At court, in list of chamberlain;
For wights near thrones care not an ace
For Wood-street friend that wieldeth mace.
Courts pay no scores but when they list,
And treasurer still has cramp in fist.
Then forth he steals, to Globe does run,
And smiles, and vows four acts are done:
Finis to bring he does protest;
Tells every player his part is best:
And all to get (as poet's use)
Some coin in pouch to solace muse.

Now wight that acts on stage of Bull,
In scullers' bark does lie at Hull,
Which he for pennies two does rig
All day on Thames to bob for grig ;
Whilst Fencer poor does by him stand
In old dung lighter, hook in hand,
Between knees rod, with canvass crib,
To girdle tied close under rib,
Where worms are put, which must small fish
Betray at night to earthen dish.

Now, London's chief on saddle new
Rides into fair of Bartholomew ;
He twirls his chain and looketh big,
As if to fright the head of pig
That gaping lies on greasy stall,
Till longing women eat it all.　　　　　[5 *w.*

Now alderman in field does stand,
With foot on trig, a quoit in hand,
"I'm seven," quoth he, " the game is up !
Nothing I pay, and yet I sup."
To alderman, quoth neighbour then,
" I lost but mutton, play for hen :"
But wealthy blade cries out, " At rate
Of kings shouldst play; let's go, 'tis late."

Now lean attorney, that his cheese
Ne'er pared, nor verses took for fees;
And aged Proctor, that controls
The feats of Poll in court of Pauls,　　　[1 *w.*
Do each with solemn oath agree
To meet in fields of Finsbury ;

With loins in canvass bow-case tied,
Where arrows stick with mickle pride;
With hats pinn'd up, and bow in hand,
All day most fiercely there they stand,
Like ghosts of Adam Bell, and Clymme :
Sol sets for fear they 'll shoot at him.

Now Spynie, Ralph, and Gregory small,
And short hair'd Stephen, whey-faced Paul,
Whose times are out, indentures torn,
Who seven long years did never scorn
To fetch up coals for maid to use,
Wipe mistresses and children's shoes,
Do jump for joy they are made free,
Hire meagre steeds, to ride and see
Their parents old, who dwell as near
As place call'd Peak in Derbyshire.
There they alight, old crones are mild,
Each weeps on crag of pretty child :
They portions give, trades up to set,
That babes may live, serve God and cheat.

Near house of law by Temple-Bar,
Now man of mace cares not how far
In stockings blue he marcheth on,
With velvet cape his cloak upon;
In girdle scrolls, where names of some
Are written down, whom touch of thumb
On shoulder left must safe convoy,
Annoying wights with name of Roy.
Poor pris'ner's friend that sees the touch
Cries out aloud, " I thought as much !"

Now vaulter good, and dancing lass
On rope, and man that cries " Ay pass !"

And tumbler young that needs but stoop,
Lay head to heel, to creep through hoop;
And man in chimney hid to dress
Puppet that acts our old Queen Bess;
And man that, whilst the puppets play,
Through nose expoundeth what they say:
And man that does in chest include
Old Sodom and Gomorrah lewd;
And white oat-eater, that does dwell
In stable small at sign of Bell,
That lifts up hoof to show the pranks
Taught by magician styled Banks;
And ape led captive still in chain,
Till he renounce the Pope and Spain.
All these on hoof now trudge from town
To cheat poor turnip-eating clown.

Now man of war with visage red
Grows choleric and swears for bread.
He sendeth note to man of kin,
But man leaves word, " I'm not within."
He meets in street with friend call'd Will,
And cries, "Old rogue! what, living still?"
But ere that street they quite are past,
He softly asks, " What money hast?"
Quoth friend, " A crown." He cries, "Dear heart!
O base no more; sweet, lend me part!"

But stay, my frighten'd pen is fled;
Myself through fear creep under bed;
For just as muse would scribble more—
Fierce city dun did rap at door.

Sir William Davenant.

PART OF AN ODE

Upon His Majesty's Proclamation (A.D. 1630) *commanding the gentry to reside upon their estates in the country.*

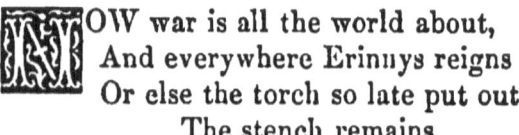OW war is all the world about,
    And everywhere Erinnys reigns
    Or else the torch so late put out,
        The stench remains.

Holland for many years hath been   .
Of Christian tragedies the stage,
Yet seldom hath she play'd a scene
        Of bloodier rage.

And France that was not long composed,
With civil drums again resounds,
And ere the old are fully closed
        Receives new wounds.

The great Gustavus in the west
Plucks the imperial eagle's wing,
Than whom the earth did ne'er invest
        A fiercer king.

What should I tell of Polish bands
And the bloods boiling in the north
'Gainst whom the furied Russians
        Their troops bring forth.

Only the island which we sow
(A world without the world) so far
From present wounds it cannot show
        An ancient scar.

White Peace (the beautifull'st of things)
Seems here her everlasting rest
To fix, and spreads her downy wings
    Over the nest.

Yet we, as if some foe were here,
Leave the despised fields to clowns,
And come to save ourselves, as 'twere
    In walled towns.

Hither we bring wives, babes, rich clothes
And gems, till now my sovereign
The growing evil doth oppose,
    Counting in vain

His care preserves us from annoy
Of enemies his realms t' invade,
Unless he force us to enjoy
    The peace he made.

To roll themselves in envied leisure
He therefore sends the landed heirs,
Whilst he proclaims not his own pleasure
    So much as theirs.

The sap and blood o' th' land, which fled
Into the root and choked the heart,
Are bid their quick'ning power to spread
    Through every part.

Oh, 'twas an act not for my muse
To celebrate, nor the dull age,
Until the country air infuse
    A purer rage.

And if the fields as thankful prove
For benefits received as seed,
They will, to 'quite so great a love,
    A Virgil breed.

A hymn that shall not cease
Th' Augustus of our world to praise
In equal verse, author of peace
    And halcyon days.
              Sir Richard Fanshawe.

A SONG TO AMORET.

I F I were dead, and in my place
    Some fresher youth design'd,
To warm thee with new fires, and grace
Those arms I left behind;

Were he as faithful as the sun
    That 's wedded to the sphere,
His blood as chaste and temp'rate run
    As April's mildest tear;

Or were he rich, and with his heaps
    And spacious share of earth
Could make divine affection cheap
    And court his golden birth;

For all these arts I'd not believe
    (No, though he should be thine)
The mighty Amorist could give
    So rich a heart as mine.

Fortune and beauty thou might'st find,
   And greater men than I;
But my true resolvèd mind
   They never shall come nigh.

For I not for an hour did love,
   Or for a day desire,
But with my soul had from above
   This endless holy fire.

Henry Vaughan.

CHLORIS AND HYLAS.

CHLORIS.

HYLAS, O Hylas, why sit we mute,
   Now that each bird saluteth the spring?
   Wind up the slacken'd strings of thy lute,
Never can'st thou want matter to sing:
For love thy breast doth fill with such a fire,
That whatsoe'er is fair moves thy desire.

HYLAS.

Sweetest, you know, the sweetest of things,
   Of various flowers the bees do compose,
Yet no particular taste it brings
   Of violet, woodbind, pink or rose:
So love the result is of all the graces
Which flow from a thousand several faces.

CHLORIS.

Hylas, the birds which chant in this grove,
   Could we but know the language they use,

They would instruct us better in love,
    And reprehend thy inconstant muse;
For Love their breasts does fill with such a fire,
That what they once do choose bounds their desire.

HYLAS.

Chloris, this change the birds do approve,
    Which the warm season hither does bring;
Time from yourself does further remove
    You than the winter from the gay spring.
She that like light'ning shined while her face lasted,
The oak now resembles which light'ning hath blasted
                                        Edmund Waller.

GRATIANA DANCING AND SINGING.

SEE! with what constant motion,
        Even and glorious as the sun,
            Gratiana steers that noble frame,
Soft as her breast, sweet as her voice,
That gave each winding law and poize,
    And swifter than the wings of fame.

She beat the happy pavement
By such a star-made firmament,
    Which now no more the roof envies;
But swells up high with Atlas even,
Bearing the brighter, nobler heaven,
    And in her all the deities.

Each step trod out a lover's thought
And the ambitious hopes he brought,
    Chained to her brave feet with such arts,

Such sweet command and gentle awe,
As when she ceased, we sighing saw
   The floor lay paved with broken hearts.

So did she move: so did she sing:
Like the harmonious spheres that bring
   Unto their rounds their music's aid;
Which she performed such a way,
As all th' enamour'd world will say,
   The Graces danced, and Apollo play'd.
                  Richard Lovelace.

THE DANCE.

BEHOLD the brand of beauty tost;
   See how the motion does dilate the flame:
      Delighted Love his spoils does boast,
   And triumph in this game.
  Fire, to no place confined,
Is both our wonder and our fear,
   Moving the mind
As lightning hurled through the air.

High heaven the glory does increase
Of all her shining lamps this artful way;
   The sun in figures, such as these,
Joys with the moon to play.
  To the sweet strains they advance
Which do result from their own spheres,
   As this nymph's dance
Moves with the numbers which she hears.
                  Edmund Waller.

HOW VIOLETS CAME BLUE.

LOVE on a day, wise poets tell,
   Some time in wrangling spent,
   Whether the violets should excel,
Or she, in sweetest scent.

But Venus having lost the day,
  Poor girls, she fell on you,
And beat ye so, as some dare say,
  Her blows did make ye blue.

Robert Herrick.

LESBIA ON HER SPARROW.

TELL me not of joys, there's none
   Now my little sparrow's gone;
    He, just as you,
    Would sigh and woo,
He would chirp and flatter me;
   He would hang the wing awhile,
   Till at length he saw me smile;
Lord! how sullen he would be!

He would catch a crumb, and then
Sporting let it go again;
    He from my lip
    Would moisture sip,
He would from my trencher feed,
   Then would hop, and then would run,
   And cry Philip when he had done;
Oh! whose heart can choose but bleed?

Oh! how eager would he fight,
And ne'er hurt though he did bite;
    No morn did pass
    But on my glass
He would sit, and mark and do
    What I did; now ruffle all
    His feathers o'er, now let them fall,
And then straightway sleek them too.

Where will Cupid get his darts
Feather'd now, to pierce our hearts?
    A wound he may,
    Not love, convey;
Now this faithful bird is gone,
    Oh! let mournful turtles join
    With loving redbreasts, and combine
To sing dirges o'er his stone.

                 William Cartwright.

FROM A BALLAD UPON A WEDDING.

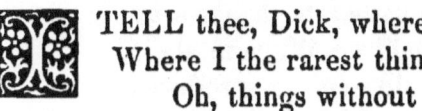 TELL thee, Dick, where I have been,
    Where I the rarest things have seen;
        Oh, things without compare!
Such sights again cannot be found
In any place on English ground,
        Be it at wake or fair.

At Charing Cross, hard by the way
Where we (thou know'st) do sell our hay,
        There is a house with stairs;
And there did I see coming down
Such folk as are not in our town,
        Vorty at least, in pairs.

Amongst the rest, one pest'lent fine,
(His beard no bigger though than thine)
          Walk'd on before the rest:
Our landlord looks like nothing to him:
The King (God bless him) 'twould undo him,
          Should he go still so dress'd.

At course-a-park, without all doubt,
He should have first been taken out
          By all the maids i' th' town:
Though lusty Roger there had been,
Or little George upon the Green,
          Or Vincent of the Crown.

But wot you what? the youth was going
To make an end of all his wooing;
          The parson for him stay'd:
Yet by his leave, for all his haste,
He did not so much wish all pass'd,
          Perchance, as did the maid.

The maid (and thereby hangs a tale)
For such a maid no Whitsun ale
          Could ever yet produce:
No grape that 's kindly ripe could be
So round, so plump, so soft as she,
          Nor half so full of juice.

Her finger was so small, the ring
Would not stay on which they did bring,
          It was too wide a peck:
And to say truth, for out it must,
It look'd like the great collar—just—
          About our young colt's neck.

Her feet beneath her petticoat,
Like little mice, stole in and out,
      As if they fear'd the light :
But oh ! she dances such a way !
No sun upon an Easter day
      Is half so fine a sight.

Her cheeks so rare a white was on,
No daisy makes comparison,
      · (Who sees them is undone)
For streaks of red were mingled there,
Such as are on a Katharine pear,
      The side that 's next the sun.

Her lips were red, and one was thin,
Compared to that was next her chin ;
      (Some bee had stung it newly).
But, Dick, her eyes so guard her face,
I durst no more upon them gaze
      Than on the sun in July.

Her mouth so small when she does speak,
Thou'dst swear her teeth her words did break,
      That they might passage get ;
But she so handled still the matter,
They came as good as ours, or better,
      And are not spent a whit.

Just in the nick the cook knock'd thrice,
And all the waiters in a trice
      His summons did obey ;
Each serving man, with dish in hand,
March'd boldly up, like our train'd band,
      Presented, and away.

When all the meat was on the table,
What man of knife or teeth was able
      To stay to be intreated?
And this the very reason was,
Before the parson could say grace,
      The company was seated.

The business of the kitchen 's great,
For it is fit that men should eat;
      Nor was it there denied:
Passion, oh me! how I run on!
There 's that that would be thought upon,
      I trow, besides the bride.

Now hats fly off, and youths carouse;
Healths first go round, and then the house,
      The Bridges came thick and thick:
And when 'twas named another's health,
Perhaps he made it her's by stealth—
      And who could help it, Dick?
              Sir John Suckling.

HERRICK ON HIMSELF.

WEARIED pilgrim I have wandered here,
Twice five-and-twenty, bate me but one year;
Long I have lasted in this world, 'tis true,
But yet those years that I have lived, but few.
Who by his gray hairs doth his lustres tell,
Lives not those years, but he that lives them well:
One man has reached his sixty years, but he
Of all those three-score has not lived half three:
He lives who lives to virtue; men who cast
Their ends for pleasure, do not live, but last.
              Robert Herrick.

THE HAG.

THE hag is astride,
 This night, for to ride,
The devil and she together;
 Through thick and through thin,
 Now out, and then in,
Though ne'er so foul be the weather.

 A thorn or a burr
 She takes for a spur;
With a lash of a bramble she rides now,
 Through brakes and through briers,
 O'er ditches and mires,
She follows the spirit that guides now.

 No beast, for his food,
 Dares now range the wood,
But hush'd in his lair he lies lurking;
 While mischiefs, by these,
 On land and on seas,
At noon of night are a working.

 The storm will arise,
 And trouble the skies,
This night; and, more for the wonder,
 The ghost from the tomb
 Affrighted shall come,
Call'd out by the clap of the thunder.
     Robert Herrick.

TO THE KING ON NEW YEAR'S DAY. 1630.

THE joys of eager youth, of wine, and wealth,
　　Of faith untroubled, and unphysick'd health;
　　　　Of lovers when their nuptial 's nigh,
　　　　Of saints forgiven when they die;
　　　　　　Let this year bring
　　　　　　To Charles our king:
　　To Charles, who is th' example and the law,
　　By whom the good are taught, not kept in awe.

Long-proffer'd peace, and that not compass'd by
Expensive treaties, but a victory;
　　　　And victories by fame obtain'd
　　　　Or prayer, and not by slaughter gain'd;
　　　　　　Let this year bring
　　　　　　To Charles our king:
　　To Charles, who is th' example and the law,
　　By whom the good are taught, not kept in awe.

A session, too, of such who can obey,
As they were gather'd to consult, not sway;
　　　　Who now rebel, in hope to get
　　　　Some office to reclaim their wit;
　　　　　　Let this year bring
　　　　　　To Charles our king:
　　To Charles who is th' example and the law,
　　By whom the good are taught, not kept in awe.

Prætors, who will the public cause defend,
With timely gifts, not speeches finely penn'd;
　　　　To make the northern victors' fame
　　　　No more our envy nor our shame;

Let this year bring
To Charles our king:
To Charles, who is th' example and the law,
By whom the good are taught, not kept in awe.

Sir W. Davenant.

TO THE QUEEN ON A NEW YEAR'S DAY.

WAKE, great Queen! for as you hide or clear
Your eyes, we shall distrust or like the year.
Queens set their dials by your beauty's light,
By your eyes learn to make their own move right;
Yet know our expectation when you rise
Is not entirely furnish'd from your eyes;
But wisely we provide how to rejoice
In the fruition of your breath and voice;
Your breath which nature the example meant,
From whence our early blossoms take their scent,
Teaching our infant flowers how to excel,
Ere strong upon their stalks, in fragrant smell;
Your voice, which can allure and charm the best
Most gaudy-feather'd chanter of the east
To dwell about your palace all the spring,
And still can make him silent whilst you sing.
Rise, then! for I have heard Apollo swear,
By that first lustre which did fill his sphere,
He will not mount, but make eternal night,
Unless relieved, and cherish'd by your sight;
Your sight, which is his warmth, now he is old,
His horses weary, and his chariot cold.

Sir W. Davenant.

BEN JONSON'S ODE TO HIMSELF UPON THE
CENSURE OF HIS "NEW INN."

JANUARY 1630.

COME, leave the loathed stage,
  And the more loathsome age ;
Where pride and impudence, in faction knit,
  Usurp the chair of wit !
Indicting and arraigning every day
  Something they call a play.
  Yet their fastidious, vain
  Commission of the brain
Run on and rage, sweat, censure and condemn :
They were not made for thee, less thou for them.

  Say that thou pour'st them wheat,
  And they will acorns eat ;
'Twere simple fury still thyself to waste
  On such as have no taste !
To offer them a surfeit of pure bread,
  Whose appetites are dead !
  No, give them grains their fill,
  Husks, draff to drink and swill :
If they love lees, and leave the lusty wine,
Envy them not, their palate 's with the swine.

  No doubt some mouldy tale,
  Like Pericles, and stale
As the shrieve's crusts, and nasty as his fish—
  Scraps, out of every dish
Thrown forth, and raked into the common tub,
  May keep up the Play-club :

There, sweepings do as well
    As the best-order'd meal;
For who the relish of these guests will fit,
Needs set them but the alms-basket of wit.

    And much good do 't to you then :
    Brave plush and velvet-men,
Can feed on orts; and, safe in your stage-clothes,
    Dare quit, upon your oaths,
The stagers and the stage-wrights too, your peers,
    Of larding your large ears
    With their foul comic socks,
    Wrought upon twenty blocks;
Which if they are torn, and turn'd, and patch'd enough,
The gamesters share your gilt, and you their stuff.

    Leave things so prostitute,
    And take the Alcaic lute,
Or thine own Horace, or Anacreon's lyre;
    Warm thee by Pindar's fire;
And though thy nerves be shrunk, and blood be cold
    Ere years have made thee old,
    Strike that disdainful heat
    Throughout, to their defeat,
As curious fools, and envious of thy strain,
May, blushing, swear no palsy 's in thy brain.

    But when they hear thee sing
    The glories of thy king,
His zeal to God, and his just awe o'er men,
    They may, blood-shaken then,
Feel such a flesh-quake to possess their powers
    As they shall cry, "Like ours,

In sound of peace or wars,
No harp e'er hit the stars,
In tuning forth the acts of his sweet reign ;
And raising Charles his chariot 'bove his wain."

Ben Jonson.

AN EPIGRAM TO KING CHARLES FOR AN HUNDRED POUNDS HE SENT ME IN MY SICKNESS. (1630.)

GREAT Charles, among the holy gifts of grace
  Annexed to thy person and thy place,
  'Tis not enough (thy piety is such)
To cure the call'd *King's-Evil* with thy touch ;
But thou wilt yet a kinglier mastery try,
To cure the *Poet's-Evil*, poverty :
And in these cures dost so thyself enlarge,
As thou dost cure our evil at thy charge.
Nay, and in this, thou show'st to value more
One poet, than of other folks ten score.
O piety, so to weigh the poor's estates !
O bounty, so to difference the rates !
What can the poet wish his king may do,
But that he cure the People's Evil too ?

Ben Jonson.

VIRTUE.

SWEET day, so cool, so calm, so bright,
  The bridal of the earth and sky,
  The dew shall weep thy fall to-night,
      For thou must die.

Sweet rose, whose hue angry and brave
Bids the rash gazer wipe his eye,
Thy root is ever in its grave,
   And thou must die.

Sweet spring, full of sweet days and roses,
A box where sweets compacted lie,
My music shows ye have your closes,
   And all must die.

Only a sweet and virtuous soul,
Like season'd timber, never gives ;
But though the whole world turn to coal,
   Then chiefly lives.
      George Herbert.

UPON THE CURTAIN OF LUCASTA'S PICTURE.

H, stay that covetous hand; first turn all eye,
 All depth and mind ; then mystically spy
 Her soul's fair picture, her fair soul's, in all
So truly copied from the original,
That you will swear her body by this law
Is but its shadow, as this its ;—now draw.
      Richard Lovelace.

THE DESCRIPTION OF CASTARA.

IKE the violet, which alone
 Prospers in some happy shade,
 My Castara lives unknown,
 To no looser eye betray'd ;
For she's to herself untrue
Who delights i' th' public view.

E

Such is her beauty, as no arts
　　Have enrich'd with borrow'd grace;
Her high birth no pride imparts,
　　For she blushes in her place;
Folly boasts a glorious blood—
She is noblest, being good.　　　　　[4 *st.*

She her throne makes reason climb,
　　Whilst wild passions captive lie;
And, each article of time,
　　Her pure thoughts to heaven fly.
All her vows religious be,
And her love she vows to me.

William Habington.

HERRICK'S CAVALIER.

IVE me that man that dares bestride
　　The active sea-horse, and with pride
　　Through that huge field of waters ride;
Who, with his looks too, can appease
The ruffling winds and raging seas
In midst of all their outrages.
This, this a virtuous man can do,
Sail against rocks, and split them too;
Ay, and a world of pikes pass through.

Robert Herrick.

TO ALTHEA FROM PRISON.

HEN love with unconfined wings
　　Hovers within my gates,
And my divine Althea brings
　　To whisper at the grates;

When I lie tangled in her hair,
  And fetter'd to her eye,
The birds, that wanton in the air,
  Know no such liberty.

When flowing cups run swiftly round
  With no allaying Thames,
Our careless heads with roses bound,
  Our hearts with loyal flames;
When thirsty grief in wine we steep,
  When healths and draughts go free,
Fishes, that tipple in the deep,
  Know no such liberty.

When—like committed linnets—I
  With shriller throat shall sing
The sweetness, mercy, majesty,
  And glories of my king;
When I shall voice aloud how good
  He is, how great should be,
Enlarged winds, that curl the flood,
  Know no such liberty.

Stone walls do not a prison make,
  Nor iron bars a cage;
Minds innocent and quiet take
  That for an hermitage;
If I have freedom in my love,
  And in my soul am free,
Angels alone that soar above
  Enjoy such liberty.

                Richard Lovelace.

TO AMARANTHA, THAT SHE WOULD
DISHEVEL HER HAIR.

MARANTHA sweet and fair,
   Ah, braid no more that shining hair !
     As my curious hand or eye,
Hovering round thee, let it fly.

   Let it fly as unconfined
As its calm ravisher, the wind,
   Who hath left his darling, th' East,
To wanton o'er that spicie nest.

   Every tress must be confest
But neatly tangled at the best,
   Like a clue of golden thread
Most excellently ravelled.

   Do not then wind up that light
In ribands, and o'er-cloud in night,
   Like the sun in 's early ray;
But shake your head, and scatter day.   [3 *st.*
                     Richard Lovelace.

TO MUSIC, TO BECALM HIS FEVER.

CHARM me asleep, and melt me so
    With thy delicious numbers,
   That being ravish'd, hence I go
Away in easy slumbers.
   Ease my sick head,
   And make my bed,

Thou power that canst sever
  From me this ill,
  And quickly still,
  Though thou not kill
    My fever.

Thou sweetly canst convert the same
  From a consuming fire
Into a gentle-licking flame,
  And make it thus expire.
    Then make me weep
    My pains asleep,
And give me such reposes,
    That I, poor I,
    May think, thereby,
    I live and die
      'Mongst roses.

Fall on me like a silent dew,
  Or like those maiden showers,
Which, by the peep of day, do strew
  A baptime o'er the flowers.
    Melt, melt my pains
    With thy soft strains,
That having ease me given,
    With full delight
    I leave this light
    And take my flight
      For heaven.
              Robert Herrick.

TIME PASSES.

TIME is a feather'd thing;
  And whilst I praise
  The sparklings of thy looks, and call them rays,
Takes wing;

Leaving behind him, as he flies,
An unperceived dimness in thine eyes.

His minutes, whilst they're told,
Do make us old,
And every sand of his fleet glass,
Increasing age as it doth pass,
Insensibly sows wrinkles there,
Where flowers and roses did appear.

Whilst we do speak, our fire
Doth into ice expire;
Flames turn to frost,
   And ere we can
   Know how our crow turns swan,
   Or how a silver snow
   Springs there where jet did grow,
Our fading spring is in dull winter lost.

Jasper Mayne.

DESIRE CHANGES.

DO'ST see how unregarded now
    That piece of beauty passes?
There was a time when I did vow
    To that alone;
  But mark the fate of faces;
The red and white works now no more on me
Than if it could not charm, or I not see;

And yet the face continues good,
    And I have still desires,
And still the self-same flesh and blood,
      As apt to melt
    And suffer from those fires;

Oh ! some kind power unriddle, where it lies,
Whether my heart be faulty or her eyes ?

She every day her man does kill,
    And I as often die ;
Neither her power then nor my will
        Can question'd be ;
    What is the mystery ?
Sure, beauties' empires, like to greater states,
Have certain periods set and hidden fates.
                  Sir John Suckling.

CHANGE OF AIR.

COME, spur away,
    I have no patience for a longer stay,
        But must go down
And leave the chargeable noise of this great town :
I will the country see
Where old simplicity,
    Though hid in grey,
    Doth look more gay
Than foppery in plush and scarlet clad.
    Farewell you city wits, that are
    Almost at civil war ;
'Tis time that I grow wise when all the world grows mad.

  More of my days
I will not spend to gain an idiot's praise ;
    Or to make sport
    For some slight puny of the inns of court.
Then, worthy Stafford, say,
How shall we spend the day ?

With what delights
Shorten the nights
When from this tumult we are got secure;
 Where mirth with all her freedom goes,
 Yet shall no finger lose;
Where every word is thought, and every thought is pure.

There, from the tree
We'll cherries pluck, and pick the strawberry;
 And every day
 Go see the wholesome girls make hay,
Whose brown hath lovelier grace
Than any painted face
 That I do know
 Hyde Park can show;
Where I had rather gain a kiss than meet
 (Though some of them, in greater state,
 Might court my love with plate)
The beauties of the Cheape, and wives of Lombard
      Street.

But think upon
Some other pleasures, these to me are none.
 Why do I prate
 Of women, that are things against my fate?
I never mean to wed
That torture to my bed.
 My muse is she
 My love shall be:
Let clowns get wealth and heirs!—when I am gone,
 And the great bugbear, grisly death,
 Shall take this idle breath,
If I a poem leave, that poem is my son.

Of this no more—
We 'll rather taste the bright Pomona's store;
 No fruit shall 'scape
 Our palates, from the damson to the grape.
Then full, we 'll seek a shade,
And hear what music 's made;
 How Philomel
 Her tale doth tell,
And how the other birds do fill the quire,
 The thrush and blackbird lend their throats
 Warbling melodious notes,
We will all sports enjoy, which others but desire.

Ours is the sky,
 Where, at what fowl we please, our hawks shall fly,
 Nor will we spare
 To hunt the crafty fox, or tim'rous hare;
  But let our hounds run loose
  In any ground they choose;
   The buck shall fall,
   The stag and all.
Our pleasures must from their own warrants be,
 For to my muse, if not to me,
 I am sure all game is free;
Heaven, earth, are all but parts of her great royalty.

And when we mean
To taste of Bacchus' blessings now and then,
And drink by stealth
A cup or two to noble Barkley's health,
 I 'll take my pipe and try
 The Phrygian melody,
  Which he that hears
  Lets through his ears

A madness to distemper all the brain.
  Then I another pipe will take,
  And Doric music make,
To civilize with graver notes our wits again.
                                    Thomas Randolph.

SONG.

HAST thou seen the down in the air,
      When wanton blasts have toss'd it?
  Or the ship on the sea,
      When ruder winds have cross'd it?
Hast thou mark'd the crocodiles weeping,
      Or the foxes sleeping?
Or hast view'd the peacock in his pride,
      Or the dove by his bride,
      When he courts for his lechery?
Oh, so fickle, oh, so vain, oh, so false, so false is she!
                                    Sir John Suckling.

JOVE'S PROPHECY IN THE HOROSCOPAL PAGEANT

Presented to Charles at his entering his city of Edinburgh, June 15, 1633.

DELIGHT of heaven! sole honour of the earth!
      Jove (courting thy ascendant) at thy birth
      Proclaimèd thee a king, and made it true,
That to thy worth great monarchies are due:
He gave thee what was good, and what was great,
What did belong to love, and what to state;

Rare gifts, whose ardours burn the hearts of all;
Like tinder, when flint's atoms on it fall.
The tramontane, which thy fair course directs,
Thy counsels shall approve by their effects;
Justice, kept low by giants, wrongs, and jars,
Thou shalt relieve, and crown with glistering stars;
Whom nought, save law of force, could keep in awe,
Thou shalt turn clients to the force of law;
Thou arms shalt brandish for thine own defence,
Wrongs to repel, and guard weak innocence,
Which to thy last effort thou shalt uphold,
As oak the ivy which it doth enfold.
All overcome, at last thyself o'ercome,
Thou shalt make Passion yield to Reason's doom:
For smiles of Fortune shall not raise thy mind,
Nor shall disasters make it e'er declined;
True Honour shall reside within thy court,
Sobriety and Truth there still resort;
Keep promised faith, thou shalt all treacheries
Detest, and fawning parasites despise;
Thou, others to make rich, shalt not make poor
Thyself, but give, that thou mayst still give more.
Thou shalt no paranymph raise to high place,
For frizzled locks, quaint pace, or painted face:
On gorgeous raiments, womanizing toys,
The works of worms, and what a moth destroys,
The maze of fools, thou shalt no treasure spend,
Thy charge to immortality shall tend;
Raise palaces, and temples vaulted high;
Rivers o'erarch; of hospitality
And sciences the ruin'd inns restore;
With walls and ports encircle Neptune's shore;
To new-found worlds thy fleets make hold their course,
And find of Canada the unknown source;

People those lands which pass Arabian fields
In fragrant woods, and musk which zephyr yields.
Thou, fear'd of none, shalt not thy people fear,
Thy people's love thy greatness shall up-rear:
Still rigour shall not shine, and mercy lower;
What love can do thou shalt not do by power;
New and vast taxes thou shalt not extort,
Load heavy those thy bounty should support.
Thou shalt not strike the hinge nor master-beam
Of thine estate; but errors in the same,
By harmless justice, graciously reform.
Delighting more in calm than roaring storm,
Thou shalt govern in peace, as did thy sire;
Keep, save thine own, and kingdoms new acquire
Beyond Alcides' pillars, and those bounds
Where Alexander gain'd the eastern crowns,
Till thou the greatest be among the Greats:
Thus heavens ordain, so have decreed the fates.

William Drummond.

ON HIS MAJESTY'S RETURN OUT OF
SCOTLAND.

WELCOME, great sir, with all the joy that's due
    To the return of peace and you.
      Two greatest blessings which this age can know;
For that to thee, for thee to heaven we owe.
      Others by war their conquests gain,
You like a god your ends obtain.
Who when rude chaos for his help did call,
Spoke but the word, and sweetly order'd all.

This happy concord in no blood is writ,
      None can grudge heaven full thanks for it;

No mothers here lament their children's fate,
And like the peace, but think it comes too late ;
      No widows hear the jocund bells,
      And take them for their husbands' knells ;
No drop of blood is spilt which might be said
To mark our joyful holiday with red.

'Twas only heaven could work this wondrous thing,
      And only work't by such a king.
Again the northern hinds may sing and plough,
And fear no harm but from the weather now.
      Again may tradesmen love their pain
      By knowing now for whom they gain.
The armour now may be hung up to sight,
And only in their halls the children fright.

The gain of civil wars will not allow
      Bay to the conqueror's brow.
At such a game what fool would venture in,
When one must lose, yet neither side can win ?
      How justly would our neighbours smile
      At these mad quarrels of our isle
Swell'd with proud hopes to snatch the whole away,
Whilst we bet all, and yet for nothing play ?   [1 *st.*

No blood so loud as that of civil war;
      It calls for dangers from afar.
Let's rather go and seek out them and fame ;
Thus our forefathers got, thus left a name.
      All their rich blood was spent with gains,
      But that which swells their children's veins.
Why sit we still, our spirits wrapt up in lead?
Not like them whilst they lived, but now they 're dead.

This noise at home was but Fate's policy
      To raise our spirits more high.

So a bold lion, ere he seeks his prey,
Lashes his sides, and roars, and then away.
      How would the German eagle fear
      To see a new Gustavus there?
How would it shake, though, as 'twas wont to do
For Jove of old, it now bore thunder too!

Sure there are actions of this height and praise
      Destined to Charles his days.
What will the triumphs of his battles be,
Whose very peace itself is victory?
      When heaven bestows the best of kings,
      It bids us think of mighty things.
His valour, wisdom, offspring, speak no less;
And we, the prophets' sons, write not by guess.
                    Abraham Cowley.

THE PERFECT LOVER.

HONEST lover whatsoever,
    If in all thy love there ever
    Was one wav'ring thought, if thy flame
Were not still even, still the same;
      Know this,
      Thou lov'st amiss,
      And to love true,
Thou must begin again, and love anew.

If when she appears i' th' room,
Thou dost not quake, and art struck dumb,
And in striving this to cover
Dost not speak thy words twice over,
      Know this,
      Thou lov'st amiss,
      And to love true,
Thou must begin again, and love anew.

If fondly thou dost not mistake,
And all defects for graces take,
Persuad'st thyself that jests are broken,
When she hath little or nothing spoken,
    Know this,
    Thou lov'st amiss,
    And to love true,
Thou must begin again, and love anew.

If when thou appearest to be within,
Thou lett'st not men ask and ask again ;
And when thou answerest, if it be
To what was ask'd thee properly,
    Know this,
    Thou lov'st amiss,
    And to love true,
Thou must begin again, and love anew.

'f when thy stomach calls to eat,
Thou cutt'st not fingers 'stead of meat,
And with much gazing on her face,
Dost not rise hungry from the place,
    Know this,
    Thou lov'st amiss,
    And to love true,
Thou must begin again, and love anew.

If by this thou dost discover
That thou art no perfect lover,
And desiring to love true,
Thou dost begin to love anew,
    Know this,
    Thou lov'st amiss,
    And to love true,
Thou must begin again, and love anew.

                  Sir John Suckling.

THE CARELESS LOVER.

NEVER believe me if I love,
  Or know what 'tis or mean to prove;
  And yet in faith I lie, I do,
And she's extremely handsome too:
    She's fair, she's wondrous fair,
    But I care not who knows it,
    Ere I'll die for love, I'll fairly forego it.

This heat of hope, or cold of fear,
My foolish heart could never bear:
One sigh imprison'd ruins more
Than earthquakes have done heretofore:
    She's fair, &c.

When I am hungry I do eat,
And cut no fingers 'stead of meat;
Nor with much gazing on her face
Do e'er rise hungry from the place:
    She's fair, &c.

A gentle round fill'd to the brink
To this and t'other friend I drink;
And when 'tis named another's health,
I never make it hers by stealth:
    She's fair, &c.

Blackfriars to me, and old Whitehall,
Is even as much as is the fall
Of fountains on a pathless grove,
And nourishes as much my love:
    She's fair, &c.

I visit, talk, do business, play,
And for a need laugh out a day :
Who does not thus in Cupid's school,
He makes not love, but plays the fool :
    She's fair, &c.
             Sir John Suckling.

SONG OF THE FAIRIES.

AT NIGHT IN AN APPLE ORCHARD.

NOS beata fauni proles,
  Quibus non est magna moles,
  Quamvis lunam incolamus,
Hortos sæpe frequentamus.

Furto cuncta magis bella,
Furto dulcior puella,
Furto omnia decora,
Furto poma dulciora.

Cum mortales lecto jacent
Nobis poma noctu placent.
Illa tamen sunt ingrata
Nisi furto sint parata.
             Thomas Randolph.

TOBACCO.

TOBACCO 's a Musician,
  And in a pipe delighteth ;
  It descends in a close,
Through the organ of the nose,
With a relish that inviteth.

F

This makes me sing So ho, ho; So ho, ho, boys,
  Ho boys, sound I loudly;
      Earth ne'er did breed
      Such a jovial weed,
  Whereof to boast so proudly.

Tobacco is a Lawyer,
  His pipes do love long cases,
      When our brains it enters
      Our feet do make indentures,
  Which we seal with stamping paces.
                    This makes me sing, &c.

Tobacco 's a Physician,
  Good both for sound and sickly;
      'Tis a hot perfume
      That expels cold rheum,
  And makes it flow down quickly.
                    This makes me sing, &c.

Tobacco is a Traveller,
  Come from the Indies hither;
      It passed sea and land
      Ere it came to my hand,
  And 'scaped the wind and weather.
                    This makes me sing, &c.

Tobacco is a Critic,
  That still old paper turneth,
      Whose labour and care
      Is as smoke in the air,
  That ascends from a rag when it burneth.
                    This makes me sing, &c.

Tobacco 's an ignis fatuus—
  A fat and fiery vapour,
    That leads men about
    Till the fire be out,
  Consuming like a taper.
             This makes me sing, &c.

Tobacco is a Whiffler,
  And cries Huff Snuff with fury ;
    His pipe's his club and link ;
    He 's the visor that does drink ;
  Thus arm'd I fear not a Jury.
             This makes me sing, &c.
                Barten Holiday.

SADNESS.

WHILES I this standing lake,
  Swathed up with yew and cypress boughs,
  Do move by sighs and vows,
  Let Sadness only wake ;
That whiles thick darkness blots the light
My thoughts may cast another night ;
  In which double shade,
  By Heaven and me made,
    O let me weep
    And fall asleep
  And forgotten fade.

  Hark ! from yond' hollow tree
Sadly sing two anchoret owls
Whiles the hermit wolf howls ;
  And all bewailing me,

The raven hovers o'er my bier,
The bittern on a reed I hear
   Pipes my elegy,
   And warns me to die.
      Whiles from yond' graves
      My wrong'd love craves
   My sad company.

Cease Hylas, cease thy call!
Such, O such, was thy parting groan,
Breathed out to me alone
   When thou, disdain'd, didst fall.
Lo thus unto thy silent tomb,
In my sad winding-sheet, I come,
   Creeping o'er dead bones
   And cold marble stones,
      That I may mourn
      Over thy urn
   And appease thy groans.

William Cartwright.

SORROW.

H, Sorrow, Sorrow, say where dost thou dwell?
   In the lowest room of hell.
   Art thou born of human race?
No, no, I have a furier face.
Art thou in city, town, or court?
   I to every place resort.
Oh, why into the world is Sorrow sent?
   Men afflicted best repent.
What dost thou feed on?
   Broken sleep.

What takest thou pleasure in?
    To weep,
    To sigh, to sob, to pine, to groan,
    To wring my hands, to sit alone.
Oh when? oh when shall Sorrow quiet have?
   Never, never, never, never.
   Never till she finds a grave.

                    Samuel Rowley.

STRAFFORD'S TRIAL AND DEATH.

REAT Strafford! worthy of that name, though all
   Of thee could be forgotten, but thy fall,
   Crush'd by imaginary treason's weight,
Which too much merit did accumulate:
As chemists gold from brass by fire would draw,
Pretexts are into treason forged by law.
His wisdom such, at once it did appear
Three kingdoms' wonder, and three kingdoms' fear;
Whilst single he stood forth, and seem'd, although
Each had an army, as an equal foe.
Such was his force of eloquence, to make
The hearers more concern'd than he that spake;
Each seem'd to act that part he came to see,
And none was more a looker-on than he;
So did he move our passions, some were known
To wish, for the defence, the crime their own.
Now private pity strove with public hate,
Reason with rage, and eloquence with fate:
Now they could him, if he could them forgive;
He's not too guilty, but too wise to live;
Less seem those facts which treason's nick-name bore,
Than such a fear'd ability for more.

They after death their fears of him express,
His innocence, and their own guilt confess.
Their legislative frenzy they repent :
Enacting it should make no precedent.
This fate he could have 'scaped, but would not lose
Honour for life, but rather nobly chose
Death from their fears, than safety from his own,
That his last action all the rest might crown.

Sir John Denham.

EPITAPH UPON THE EARL OF STRAFFORD.

(BEHEADED MAY 12TH, 1641.)

ERE lies wise and valiant dust,
　　Huddled up 'twixt fit and just :
　　Strafford, who was hurried hence
'Twixt treason and convenience.
He spent his time here in a mist,
A papist yet a calvinist.
His prince's nearest joy and grief,
He had, yet wanted, all relief :
The prop and ruin of the state,
The people's violent love and hate.
One in extremes loved and abhorr'd.
Riddles lie here, and in a word
Here lies blood, and let it lie
Speechless still, and never cry.

John Cleveland.

THE FALL.

HE bloody trunk of him who did possess
　　Above the rest a hapless happy state
　　This little stone doth seal, but not depress,
And scarce can stop the rolling of his fate.

Brass tombs which justice hath denied to his fault
  The common pity to his virtues pays,
Adorning on imaginary vault
  Which from our minds Time strives in vain to raze.

Ten years the world upon him falsely smiled,
  Sheathing in fawning looks the deadly knife
Long aimed at his head; that so beguiled
  It more securely might bereave his life;

Then threw him to a scaffold from a throne.
  Much doctrine lies under this little stone.

Sir Richard Fanshawe.

THE VINTAGE TO THE DUNGEON.

ING out, pent souls, sing cheerfully!
  Care shackles you in liberty:
  Mirth frees you in captivity.
    Would you double fetters add?
    Else why so sad?

Chorus.

Besides your pinion'd arms you 'll find
Grief too can manacle the mind.

Live then, prisoners, uncontroled;
Drink o' the strong, the rich, the old,
Till wine too hath your wits in hold;
    Then if still your jollity
    And throats are free—

Chorus.

Triumph in your bonds and pains,
And dance to the music of your chains.

Richard Lovelace.

COURANTE MONSIEUR.

HAT frown, Aminta, now hath drown'd
    Thy bright front's power, and crown'd
      Me that was bound.
No, no, deceived cruel, no!
      Love's fiery darts,
Till tipt with kisses, never kindle hearts.

Adieu, weak beauteous tyrant, see!
    Thy angry flames, meant me,
      Retort on thee:
For know, it is decreed, proud fair,
      I ne'er must die
By any scorching, but a melting eye.

                Richard Lovelace.

DISDAIN RETURNED.

E that loves a rosy cheek,
    Or a coral lip admires,
      Or from star-like eyes doth seek
    Fuel to maintain his fires;
As old time makes these decay,
    So his flames must waste away.

But a smooth and steadfast mind,
    Gentle thoughts, and calm desires,
Hearts with equal love combined,
    Kindle never-dying fires.
Where these are not, I despise
Lovely cheeks, or lips, or eyes.   [1 *st.*

                Thomas Carew.

LOVE'S GOOD MORROW.

PACK clouds away, and welcome day,
   With night we banish sorrow;
  Sweet air blow soft, larks mount aloft,
  To give my love good-morrow.
Wings from the wind to please her mind,
  Notes from the lark I'll borrow;
Bird prune thy wing, nightingale sing,
  To give my love good-morrow,
  Notes from them both I'll borrow.

Wake from thy nest, robin-red-breast,
  Sing birds in every furrow;
And from each hill let music shrill
  Give my fair love good-morrow.
Blackbird, and thrush, in every bush,
  Stare, linnet, and cock-sparrow!
You pretty elves, among yourselves,
  Sing my fair love good-morrow.
  To give my love good-morrow,
  Sing birds in every furrow.

                Thomas Heywood.

A KING AND NO KING.

THAT prince who may do nothing but what 's just,
  Rules but by leave, and takes his crown on
    trust.

                Robert Herrick

MAN'S MEDLEY.

HARK, how the birds do sing,
  And woods do ring.
All creatures have their joy, and man hath his.
 Yet if we rightly measure,
  Man's joy and pleasure
Rather hereafter, than in present, is.

 To this life things of sense
  Make their pretence :
In the other angels have a right by birth :
 Man ties them both alone,
  And makes them one,
With the one hand touching heaven, with the other earth.

 Not, that he may not here   [1 *st.*
  Taste of the cheer :
But as birds drink, and straight lift up their head ;
 So must he sip, and think
  Of better drink
He may attain to, after he is dead.

 But as his joys are double,
  So is his trouble.
He hath two winters, other things but one :
 Both frosts and thoughts do nip,
  And bite his lip ;
And he of all things fears two deaths alone.

 Yet even the greatest griefs
  May be reliefs,
Could he but take them right, and in their ways.
 Happy is he, whose heart
  Hath found the art
To turn his double pains to double praise.
       George Herbert.

CARE'S CURE.

APPY is that state of his
  Takes the world as it is,
    Lose he honours, friendship, wealth,
Lose he liberty or health,
Lose he all that earth can give,
Having nought whereon to live;
So prepared a mind's in him,
He's resolved to sink or swim.   [2 *st.*

Should I ought dejected be,
'Cause blind Fortune frowns on me?
Or put finger in the eye
When I see my Damon die?
Or repine such should inherit
More of honours than of merit?
Or put on a sourer face,
To see virtue in disgrace?   [1 *st.*

Should I weep when I do try
Fickle friends' inconstancy,
Quite discarding mine and me,
When they should the firmest be,
Or think much when barren brains
Are possess'd of rich domains,
When in reason it were fit
They had wealth unto their wit?   [3 *st.*

Should I sigh, because I see
Laws like spider-webs to be,
Lesser flies are quickly ta'en,
While the great break out again;

Or so many schisms and sects,
Which foul heresy detects,
To suppress the fire of zeal
Both in Church and Common-weal ?   [7 *st.*

No, there's nought on earth I fear
That may force from me one tear.
Loss of honour, freedom, health,
Or that mortal idol, wealth :
With these, babes may grieved be,
But they have no power on me.
Less my substance, less my share
In my fear and in my care.   [3 *st.*

Thus to love, and thus to live,
Thus to take, and thus to give ;
Thus to laugh, and thus to sing,
Thus to mount on pleasure's wing ;
Thus to sport, and thus to speed,
Thus to flourish, nourish, feed ;
Thus to spend, and thus to spare
Is to bid, *a fig for Care.*

Richard Brathwaite.

TO AMORET.

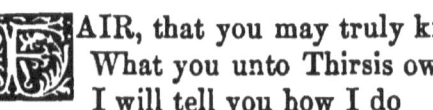AIR, that you may truly know
What you unto Thirsis owe,
I will tell you how I do
Sacharissa love and you.
Joy salutes me, when I set
My bless'd eyes on Amoret :
But with wonder I am strook,
While I on the other look.
If sweet Amoret complains,
I have sense of all her pains ;

But for Sacharissa I
Do not only grieve, but die.
All that of myself is mine,
Lovely Amoret, is thine;
Sacharissa's captive fain
Would untie his iron chain:
And those scorching beams to shun,
To thy gentle shadow run.
If the soul had free election
To dispose of her affection,
I would not thus long have borne
Haughty Sacharissa's scorn:
But 'tis sure some power above,
Which controls our wills in love,
If not love, a strong desire
To create and spread that fire,
In my breast solicits me,
Beauteous Amoret, for thee.
'Tis amazement more than love,
Which her radiant eyes do move;
If less splendour wait on thine,
Yet they so benignly shine,
I would turn my dazzled sight
To behold their milder light.
But as hard 'tis to destroy
That high flame, as to enjoy:
Which, how easily I may do
Heav'n (as easily scaled) does know.
Amoret's as sweet and good
As the most delicious food,
Which but tasted, does impart
Life and gladness to the heart:
Sacharissa's beauty's wine,
Which to madness doth incline;

Such a liquor as no brain
That is mortal, can sustain.
Scarce can I to heaven excuse
The devotion which I use
Unto that adored dame;
For 'tis not unlike the same,
Which I thither ought to send;
So that if it could take end,
'T would to heaven itself be due
To succeed her, and not you,
Who already have of me
All that's not idolatry;
Which, though not so fierce a flame,
Is longer like to be the same.
Then smile on me, and I will prove
Wonder is shorter lived than love.

Edmund Waller.

WISHES, TO HIS SUPPOSED MISTRESS.

WHOE'ER she be,
     That not impossible she,
     That shall command my heart and me :

Where'er she lie,
Lock'd up from mortal eye,
In shady leaves of destiny :

Till that ripe birth
Of studied fate stand forth
And teach her fair steps to our earth :

Till that divine
Idea take a shrine
Of crystal flesh, through which to shine :

Meet you her, my wishes,
Bespeak her to my blisses,
And be ye call'd my absent kisses.

I wish her beauty,
That owes not all its duty
To gaudy tire, or glist'ring shoe-tie.   [2 *st.*

A face, that's best
By its own beauty dress'd,
And can alone command the rest.   [2 *st.*

A cheek, where grows
More than a morning rose,
Which to no box his being owes.

Lips, where all day
A lover's kiss may play,
Yet carry nothing thence away.   [1 *st.*

Eyes, that displace
The neighbour diamond, and out-face
That sunshine by their own sweet grace.

Tresses that wear
Jewels, but to declare
How much themselves more precious are.   [2 *st.*

A well-tamed heart,
For whose more noble smart
Love may be long choosing a dart.   [6 *st.*

Days, that need borrow
No part of their good morrow,
From a forespent night of sorrow.

Days, that in spite
Of darkness, by the light
Of a clear mind, are day all night.   [1 *st.*

Life, that dares send
A challenge to his end,
And when it comes, say, Welcome, friend !

Sydneian showers
Of sweet discourse, whose powers
Can crown old winter's head with flowers.

Soft silken hours,
Open suns, shady bowers,
'Bove all—nothing within that lowers.   [3 *st.*

I wish her store
Of worth may leave her poor
Of wishes ; and I wish——no more.

Now, if Time knows
That her, whose radiant brows
Weave them a garland of my vows ;   [1 *st.*

Her, that dares be
What these lines wish to see :
I seek no further, it is she.   [2 *st.*

Such worth as this is
Shall fix my flying wishes,
And determine them to kisses.

Let her full glory,
My fancies, fly before ye,
Be ye my fictions but her story.

                             Richard Crashaw.

MONTROSE'S LOVE.

M Y dear and only love, I pray
  That little world,—of THEE,—
Be govern'd by no other sway
Than purest Monarchy.
For if confusion have a part,
 Which virtuous souls abhor,
I'll call a Synod in mine heart,
 And never love thee more.

As Alexander I will reign,
 And I will reign alone ;
My soul did evermore disdain
 A rival on my throne.
He either fears his fate too much,
 Or his deserts are small,
That dares not put it to the touch
 To gain or lose it all.   [*1 st.*

And in the Empire of thy heart,
 Where I should solely be,
If others do pretend a part,
 Or dare to vie with me,
Or Committees if thou erect,
 And go on such a score,
I'll laugh and sing at thy neglect,
 And never love thee more.

But if thou wilt prove faithful then,
 And constant of thy word,
I'll make thee glorious by my pen,
 And famous by my sword.

G

I'll serve thee in such noble ways
 Was never heard before;
I'll crown and deck thee all with bays,
 And love thee more and more.

    Marquis of Montrose.

A LOVER'S ABSENCE.

TO carve our loves in myrtle rinds
 And tell our secrets to the woods,
 To send our sighs by faithful winds,
 And trust our tears unto the floods;
To call where no man hears,
And think that rocks have ears;
To walk and rest, to live and die,
And yet not know whence, how or why;
To have our hopes with fears still check'd,
To credit doubts, and truth suspect;
 This, this is that we may
 A lover's absence say.
Follies without, are cares within;
Where eyes do fail, there souls begin.

    William Cartwright.

THE MESSAGE OF THE ROSE.

O, lovely rose,
 Tell her that wastes her time and me,
 That now she knows
When I resemble her to thee
How sweet and fair she seems to be.

Tell her that 's young,
And shuns to have her grace spy'd,
   That hadst thou sprung
In deserts, where no men abide,
Thou must have uncommended died.

   Small is the worth
Of beauty from the light retired ;
   Bid her come forth;
Suffer her self to be desired,
And not blush so to be admired.

   Then die, that she
The common fate of all things rare
   May read in thee :
How small a part of time they share,
That are so wond'rous sweet and fair.

Edmund Waller.

TO DAFFODILS.

FAIR Daffodils, we weep to see
   You haste away so soon ;
As yet the early-rising sun
Has not attain'd his noon.
     Stay, stay,
   Until the hasting day
       Has run
   But to the even-song ;
And, having pray'd together, we
   Will go with you along.

We have short time to stay, as you,
    We have as short a spring;
As quick a growth to meet decay,
    As you, or any thing.
            We die,
    As your hours do, and dry
            Away,
    Like to the summer's rain;
Or as the pearls of morning's dew,
    Ne'er to be found again.

                                Robert Herrick.

THE NIGHTINGALE.

WEET bird, that sing'st away the early hours
    Of winters past, or coming void of care,
        Well pleased with delights which present are,
Fair seasons, budding sprays, sweet-smelling flowers:
To rocks, to springs, to rills, from leafy bowers
Thou thy Creator's goodness dost declare
And what dear gifts on thee he did not spare,
A stain to human sense in sin that lowers.
What soul can be so sick, which by thy songs
(Attired in sweetness) sweetly is not driven
Quite to forget earth's turmoils, spites, and wrongs,
And lift a reverent eye and thought to heaven?
    Sweet, artless songster, thou my mind dost raise
    To airs of spheres, yes, and to angels' lays.

                                William Drummond.

TO HENRY LAWES.

TOUCH but thy lyre, my Harry, and I hear
    From thee some raptures of the rare Gotire;
    Then if thy voice commingle with the string,
I hear in thee the rare Laniere to sing;
Or curious Wilson: Tell me, canst thou be
Less than Apollo, that usurp'st such three?
Three, unto whom the whole world give applause;
Yet their three praises, praise but one; that's Lawes.

Robert Herrick.

LITANY TO THE HOLY SPIRIT.

IN the hour of my distress,
    When temptations me oppress,
    And when I my sins confess,
        Sweet Spirit, comfort me!

When I lie within my bed,
Sick in heart, and sick in head,
And with doubts discomforted,
        Sweet Spirit, comfort me!

When the house doth sigh and weep,
And the world is drown'd in sleep,
Yet mine eyes the watch do keep;
        Sweet Spirit, comfort me!

When the artless doctor sees
No one hope, but of his fees,
And his skill runs on the lees,
        Sweet Spirit, comfort me!   [1 *st.*

When the passing bell doth toll,
And the furies in a shoal
Come to fright a parting soul,
        Sweet Spirit, comfort me!

When the tapers now burn blue,
And the comforters are few,
And that number more than true,
        Sweet Spirit, comfort me!

When the priest his last hath pray'd,
And I nod to what is said,
'Cause my speech is now decay'd,
        Sweet Spirit, comfort me!

When, God knows, I'm tost about,
Either with despair or doubt;
Yet, before the glass be out,
        Sweet Spirit, comfort me!

When the tempter me pursu'th
With the sins of all my youth,
And half damns me with untruth;
        Sweet Spirit, comfort me!

When the flames and hellish cries
Fright mine ears, and fright mine eyes,
And all terrors me surprise;
        Sweet Spirit, comfort me!

When the Judgment is reveal'd,
And that open'd which was seal'd,
When to Thee I have appeal'd;
        Sweet Spirit, comfort me!

Robert Herrick.

THE ARREST OF THE FIVE MEMBERS.

(*January*, 1641-2.)

To the Five Members of the Honourable House of Commons.

The Humble Petition of the Poets.

AFTER so many concurring petitions
From all ages and sexes, and all conditions,
We come in the rear to present our follies
To Pym, Stroude, Haslerig, Hampden, and Hollis;
Though set form of prayer be an abomination,
Set forms of petitions find great approbation :
Therefore, as others from the bottom of their souls,
So we from the depth and bottom of our bowls,
According unto the bless'd form you have taught us,
We thank you first for the ills you have brought us :
For the good we receive we thank him that gave it,
And you for the confidence only to crave it.
Next in course, we complain of the great violation
Of privilege (like the rest of our nation)
But 'tis none of yours of which we have spoken,
Which never had being, until they were broken;
But ours is a privilege ancient and native,
Hangs not on an ordinance, or power legislative.
And first, 'tis to speak whatever we please
Without fear of a prison or pursuivants' fees.
Next, that we only may lie by authority,
But in that also you have got the priority.
Next, an old custom, our fathers did name it
Poetical licence, and always did claim it.

By this we have power to change age into youth,
Turn nonsense to sense, and falsehood to truth;
In brief, to make good whatsoever is faulty,
This art some poet, or the devil has taught ye:
And this our property you have invaded,
And a privilege of both Houses have made it.
But that trust above all in poets reposed,
That kings by them only are made and deposed,
This though you cannot do, yet you are willing;
But when we undertake deposing or killing,
They 're tyrants and monsters, and yet then the poet
Takes full revenge on the villains that do it:
And when we resume a sceptre or a crown,
We are modest, and seek not to make it our own.
But is 't not presumption to write verses to you,
Who make the better poems of the two?
For all those pretty knacks you compose,
Alas, what are they but poems in prose?
And between those and ours there 's no difference,
But that yours want the rhyme, the wit and the sense:
But for lying (the most noble part of a poet)
You have it abundantly, and yourselves know it,
And though you are modest, and seem to abhor it,
'T has done you good service, and thank hell for it:
Although the old maxim remains still in force,
That a sanctified cause must have a sanctified course.
If poverty be a part of our trade,
So far the whole kingdom poets you have made,
Nay even so far as undoing will do it,
You have made king Charles himself a poet:
But provoke not his muse, for all the world knows,
Already you have had too much of his prose.

Sir John Denham.

THE SAINT'S ENCOURAGEMENT.

(*Written in* 1643.)

FIGHT on, brave soldiers, for the cause!
    Fear not the Cavaliers!
    Their threatenings are as senscless, as
  Our jealousies and fears.
'Tis you must perfect this great work
  And all malignants slay,
You must bring back the King again
  The clean contrary way.

'Tis for religion that you fight,
  And for the kingdom's good ;
By robbing churches, plundering men,
  And shedding guiltless blood.
Down with the orthodoxal train,
  All loyal subjects slay ;
When these are gone we shall be blest
  The clean contrary way.   [1 *st.*

'Tis to preserve his Majesty,
  That we against him fight,
Nor are we ever beaten back,
  Because our cause is right.
If any make a scruple on 't,
  Our declarations say,
Who fight for us, fight for the King,
  The clean contrary way.

At Keinton, Brentford, Plymouth, York,
  And divers places more,
What victories we saints obtain'd !
  The like ne'er seen before.

How often we Prince Rupert kill'd,
  And bravely won the day,
The wicked cavaliers did run
  The clean contrary way.   [1 st.

We subjects' liberties preserve
  By prisonment and plunder,
And do enrich ourselves and state
  By keeping the wicked under.
We must preserve mechanics now,
  To lecturize and pray;
By them the gospel is advanced,
  The clean contrary way.

And though the King be much misled
  By that malignant crew;
He'll find us honest, and at last,
  Give all of us our due.   [8 ll.
But when our faith and works fall down,
  And all our hopes decay,
Our acts will bear us up to heaven,
  The clean contrary way.

                    Alexander Brome.

A BILL OF FARE.

EXPECT no strange or puzzling meat, nor pie
  Built by confusion or adultery
  Of forced nature; no mysterious dish
Requiring an interpreter, no fish
Found out by modern luxury: Our coarse board
Press'd with no spoils of elements, doth afford
Meat, like our hunger, without art, each mess
Thus differing from it only, that 'tis less.

  Imprimis, some rice porridge, sweet, and hot,
Three knobs of sugar season the whole pot.

Item, one pair of eggs in a great dish,
So order'd that they cover all the fish.

Item, one gaping haddock's head, which will
At least affright the stomach, if not fill.

Item, one thing in circles, which we take
Some for an eel, but th' wiser for a snake.

We have not still the same, sometimes we may
Eat muddy plaice, or wheat; perhaps next day
Red or white herrings, or an apple pie:
There's some variety in misery.

To this come twenty men, and, though apace
We bless these gifts, the meal's as short as grace.
Nor eat we yet in tumult; but the meat
Is broke in order.   Hunger here is neat;
Division, subdivision, yet two more
Members, and they divided, as before.
O what a fury would your stomach feel
To see us vent our logic on an eel,
And in one herring to revive the art
Of Keckerman and show the eleventh part?
Hunger in arms is no great wonder, we
Suffer a siege without an enemy.
On Midlent Sunday, when the preacher told
The prodigal's return, and did unfold
His tender welcome, how the good old man
Sent for new raiment, how the servant ran
To kill the fatling calf, O how each ear
Listen'd unto him, greedy ev'n to hear
The bare relation; how was every eye
Fix'd on the pulpit; how did each man pry
And watch, if, whiles he did this word dispense,
A capon or a hen would fly out thence!

Happy the Jews, cry we, when quails came down
In dry and wholesome showers, though from the frown
Of Heaven sent, though bought at such a rate ;
To perish full is not the worst of fate.
We fear we shall die empty, and enforce
The grave to take a shadow for a corse:
For, if this fasting hold, we do despair
Of life ; all needs must vanish into air—
Air which now only feeds us—and so be
Exhaled like vapours to eternity.
W' are much refined already, that dull house
Of clay (our body) is diaphanous ;
And if the doctor would but take the pains
To read upon us, sinews, bones, guts, veins,
All would appear, and he might show each one,
Without the help of a dissection.

In the abundance of this want, you will
Wonder, perhaps, how I can use my quill?
Troth I am like small birds, which, now in spring,
When they have nought to Eat do sit and Sing.

William Cartwright.

PERSUASIONS TO LOVE.

HESE curious locks, so aptly twined,   [36 *ll.*
Whose every hair a soul doth bind,
Will change their auburn hue, and grow
White, and cold as winter's snow.
That eye which now is Cupid's nest
Will prove his grave, and all the rest
Will follow ; in the cheek, chin, nose,
Nor lily shall be found, nor rose.
And what will then become of all

Those, whom you now servants call?
Like swallows, when your summer's done,
They'll fly and seek some warmer sun.
Then wisely choose one to your friend,
Whose love may (when your beauties end)
Remain still firm : be provident
And think before the summer's spent
Of following winter ; like the ant
In plenty hoard for time of scant.
Cull out amongst the multitude
Of lovers, that seek to intrude
Into your favour, one that may
Love for an age, not for a day.
For when the storms of time have moved
Waves on that cheek which was beloved,
When a fair lady's face is pined,
And yellow spread where red once shined,
When beauty, youth, and all sweets leave her,
Love may return, but lover never!   [18 *ll.*

Thomas Carew.

TO HIS FELLOW POET.

HEN we are dead, and now, no more
Our harmless mirth, our wit, and score
Distracts the Town ; when all is spent
That the base niggard world hath lent
Thy purse, or mine ; when the loath'd noise
Of drawers, prentices and boys
Hath left us, and the clam'rous bar
Items no pints i' th' Moon, or Star ;
When no calm whisperers wait the doors,
To fright us with forgotten scores ;
And such aged, long bills carry,

As might start an antiquary;
When the sad tumults of the maze,
Arrests, suits, and the dreadful face
Of serjeants are not seen, and we
No lawyer's ruffs or gowns must fee :
When all these mulcts are paid, and I
From thee, dear wit, must part, and die;
We'll beg the world would be so kind
To give's one grave, as we'd one mind ;
There (as the wiser few suspect,
That spirits after death affect)
Our souls shall meet, and thence will they
(Freed from the tyranny of clay)
With equal wings and ancient love
Into the Elysian fields remove,
Where in those blessed walks they'll find,
More of thy genius, and my mind.   [30 *ll.*

Henry Vaughan.

SPRING SUN.

NEW doth the sun appear,
   The mountains' snows decay,
     Crown'd with frail flowers forth comes the
       infant year ;
My soul, Time posts away,
And thou yet in that frost
Which flower and fruit hath lost,
As if all here immortal were, dost stay ;
For shame ! thy powers awake,
Look to that Heaven which never night makes black,
And there, at that immortal sun's bright rays,
Deck thee with flowers which fear not rage of days.

William Drummond.

A WESTERN WONDER.

DO you not know, not a fortnight ago,
    How they bragg'd of a western wonder?
    When a hundred and ten slew five thousand men ,
With the help of lightning and thunder?

There Hopton was slain, again and again,
    Or else my author did lie;
With a new thanksgiving, for the dead who are living,
    To God, and his servant Chidleigh.

But now on which side was this miracle try'd,
    I hope we at last are even;
For Sir Ralph and his knaves are risen from their graves,
    To cudgel the clowns of Devon.

And there Stamford came, for his honour was lame
    Of the gout three months together;
But it proved, when they fought, but a running gout,
    For his heels were lighter than ever.

For now he out-runs his arms and his guns,
    And leaves all his money behind him.
But they follow after, unless he take water,
    At Plymouth again, they will find him.

What Reading hath cost, and Stamford hath lost,
    Goes deep in the sequestrations;
These wounds will not heal, with your new great seal,
    Nor Jephson's declarations.

Now Peters, and Case, in your prayer and grace
    Remember the new thanksgiving;
Isaac and his wife, now dig for your life,
    Or shortly, you'll dig for your living.
                  Sir John Denham.

THE SOLDIER GOING TO THE FIELD.

PRESERVE thy sighs, unthrifty girl,
    To purify the air ;
Thy tears to thread, instead of pearls,
    On bracelets of thy hair.

The trumpet makes the echo hoarse,
    And wakes the louder drum ;
Expense of grief gains no remorse
    When sorrow should be dumb.

For I must go where lazy Peace
    Will hide her drowsy head ;
And, for the sport of kings, increase
    The number of the dead.

But first I'll chide thy cruel theft :
    Can I in war delight,
Who, being of my heart bereft,
    Can have no heart to fight ?

Thou know'st the sacred laws of old
    Ordain'd a thief should pay,
To quit him of his theft, sevenfold
    What he had stolen away.

Thy payment shall but double be ;
    O then with speed resign
My own seduced heart to me,
    Accompanied with thine.

Sir W. Davenant.

TWO HEARTS.

PRITHEE send me back my heart,
Since I cannot have thine :
For if from yours you will not part,
Why then shouldst thou have mine ?

Yet now I think on't, let it lie,
To find it were in vain,
For th' hast a thief in either eye
Would steal it back again.

Why should two hearts in one breast lie,
And yet not lodge together ?
Oh, Love, where is thy sympathy,
If thus our breasts thou sever !

But love is such a mystery,
I cannot find it out :
For when I think I'm best resolved,
I then am in most doubt.

Then farewell care, and farewell woe,
I will no longer pine,
For I'll believe I have her heart
As much as she hath mine.

Sir John Suckling.

UPON KINGS.

KINGS must be dauntless ; subjects will contemn
Those who want hearts, and wear a diadem.

Robert Herrick.

TO LIVE MERRILY, AND TO TRUST TO
GOOD VERSES.

OW is the time for mirth,
    Nor cheek or tongue be dumb;
For with flowery earth,
    The golden pomp is come.

The golden pomp is come;
    For now each tree does wear
(Made of her pap and gum)
    Rich beads of Amber here.

Now reigns the Rose, and now
    Th' Arabian dew besmears
My uncontrolled brow,
    And my retorted hairs.

Homer, this health to thee,
    In sack of such a kind,
That it would make thee see,
    Though thou wert ne'er so blind.

Next, Virgil, I'll call forth,
    To pledge this second health
In wine, whose each cup 's worth
    An Indian commonwealth.

A goblet next I 'll drink
    To Ovid; and suppose
Made he the pledge, he 'd think
    The world had all one Nose.

WITH THE KING.

Then this immensive cup
   Of Aromatic wine,
Catullus, I quaff up
   To that terse muse of thine.

Wild I am now with heat;
   O Bacchus! cool thy rays,
Or frantic I shall eat
   Thy Thyrse, and bite the bays.

Round, round, the roof does run;
   And being ravish'd thus,
Come, I will drink a tun
   To my Propertius.

Now, to Tibullus, next,
   This flood I drink to thee:
But stay; I see a Text,
   That this presents to me.

Behold, Tibullus lies
   Here burnt, whose small return
Of ashes, scarce suffice
   To fill a little urn.

Trust to good Verses then;
   They only will aspire,
When pyramids, as men,
   Are lost i' th' funeral fire.

And when all bodies meet
   In Lethe, to be drown'd;
Then only Numbers sweet
   With endless life are crown'd.

                Robert Herrick.

OBEDIENCE.

THE power of princes rests in the consent
Of only those who are obedient;
Which if away, proud sceptres then will lie
Low, and of thrones the ancient majesty.

Robert Herrick.

TO THE KING ON HIS COMING WITH AN ARMY INTO THE WEST.

WELCOME, most welcome to our vows and us,
Most great and universal Genius!
The drooping West, which hitherto has stood
As one in long-lamented widowhood,
Looks like a bride now, or a bed of flowers,
Newly refresh'd both by the sun and showers;
War, which before was horrid, now appears
Lovely in you, brave Prince of Cavaliers!
A deal of courage in each bosom springs
By your access, O you the best of kings!
Ride on with all white omens, so that where
Your standard's up, we fix a conquest there.

Robert Herrick.

KINGS AND TYRANTS.

TWIXT kings and tyrants there's this difference
known,
Kings seek their subjects' good, tyrants their
own. *Robert Herrick.*

TO THE KING, UPON HIS TAKING OF LEICESTER.

(*May* 31, 1645.)

THIS day is yours, great Charles! and in this war
Your fate and ours alike victorious are.
In her white stole now Victory does rest,
Ensphered with palm on your triumphant crest;
Fortune is now your captive; other kings
Hold but her hands; you hold both hands and wings.

Robert Herrick.

THE DOWNFALL OF CHARING CROSS.

UNDONE, undone, the lawyers are;
  They wander about the town;
 Nor can find the way to Westminster,
  Now Charing Cross is down:
At the end of the Strand they make a stand,
  Swearing they are at a loss,
And chaffing say, that's not the way,
  They must go by Charing Cross.

The Parliament to vote it down
  Conceived it very fitting,
For fear it should fall, and kill them all
  In the house, as they were sitting.
They were told, god-wot, it had a plot,
  Which made them so hard-hearted,
To give command it should not stand,
  But be taken down and carted.

Men talk of plots ; this might have been worse
    For anything I know,
Than that Tomkins and Chaloner
    Were hang'd for long ago.
Our Parliament did that prevent,
    And wisely them defended,
For plots they will discover still,
    Before they were intended.

But neither man, woman, nor child,
    Will say, I'm confident,
They ever heard it speak one word
    Against the Parliament.
An informer swore, it letters bore,
    Or else it had been freed ;
I'll take, in troth, my Bible oath
    It could neither write nor read.

The Committee said, that verily
    To Popery it was bent ;
For aught I know, it might be so,
    For to church it never went.
What with excise, and such device,
    The kingdom doth begin
To think you 'll leave them ne'er a cross,
    Without doors nor within.

Methinks the Common-council should
    Of it have taken pity,
'Cause, good old cross, it always stood
    So firmly to the city.
Since crosses you so much disdain,
    Faith, if I were as you,
For fear the king should rule again,
    I 'd pull down Tyburn too.

                          Percy Reliques.

ON THE LOSS OF A GARRISON, MEDITATION.

ANOTHER city lost! alas poor King!
Still future griefs from former griefs do spring.
The world's a seat of change; kingdoms and Kings
Though glorious, are but sublunary things.
Crosses and blessings kiss; there's none that be
So happy, but they meet with misery.
He that erewhile sat centered to his throne,
And all did homage unto him alone;
Who did the sceptre of his power display
From pole to pole, while all this rule obey,
From stair to stair now tumbles, tumbles down,
And scarce one pillar doth support his crown.
Town after town, field after field,
This turns, and that perfidiously doth yield:
He's banded on the traitorous thought of those
That, Janus like, look to him and his foes.
In vain are bulwarks, and the strongest hold,
If the besieger's bullets are of gold.
My soul, be not dejected; would'st thou be
From present trouble or from danger free?
Trust not in rampires, nor the strength of walls,
The town that stands to-day to-morrow falls.
Trust not in soldiers, though they seem so stout;
When sin's within, vain is defence without.
Trust not in wealth, for in this lawless time
Where prey is penalty, there wealth is crime.
Trust not in strength or courage; we all see
The weakest ofttimes do gain the victory.
Trust not in honour, honour's but a blast
Quickly begun, and but a while doth last.

They that to-day to thee Hosanna cry,
To-morrow change their note for Crucify !
Trust not in friends, for friends will soon deceive thee,
They are in nothing sure, but sure to leave thee.
Trust not in wits, who run from place to place
Changing religion as chance does her face ;
In spite of cunning, and their strength of brain,
They 're often catch, and all their plots are vain.
Trust not in council ; potentates or kings
All are but frail and transitory things.
Since neither soldiers, castles, wealth or wit,
Can keep off harm from thee, or thee from it :
Since neither strength nor honour, friends nor lords,
Nor princes, peace or happiness affords,

  Trust thou in God, ply Him with prayers still,
  Be sure of help ; for He both can and will.

        Alexander Brome.

THE COMMONERS.

(*Written in* 1645.)

OME your ways,
 Bonny boys
  Of the town,
For now is your time or never.
 Shall your fears
 Or your cares
  Cast you down ?
Hang your wealth
And your health
  Get renown,
We are all undone for ever.
Now the King and the Crown
Are tumbling down,

And the realm doth groan with disasters,
　　And the scum of the land
　　Are the men that command,
And our slaves are become our masters.

　　　　Now our lives,
　　　　Children, wives,
　　　　　　And estate,
　　Are a prey to the lust and plunder,
　　　　To the rage
　　　　Of our age.
　　　　　　And the fate
　　　　Of our land
　　　　Is at hand,
　　　　　　'Tis too late
　　To tread these usurpers under.
　　First down goes the crown,
　　Then follows the gown;
Thus levelled are we by the Roundhead,
　　While Church and State must
　　Feed their pride and their lust,
And the Kingdom and King be confounded.

　　　　Shall we still
　　　　Suffer ill,
　　　　　　And be dumb?
　　And let every varlet undo us?
　　　　Shall we doubt
　　　　Of each lout,
　　　　　　That doth come,
　　　　With a voice
　　　　Like the noise
　　　　　　Of a drum,
　　And a sword or a buff-coat to us?

Shall we lose our estates
By plunder and rates
To bedeck those proud upstarts that swagger?
Rather fight for your meat,
Which these locusts do eat,
Now every man's a beggar.

Alexander Brome.

THE ROYALIST.

(*Written in* 1646.)

OME pass about the bowl to me,
A health to our distressed King;
Though we 're in hold, let cups go free,
Birds in a cage may freely sing.
The ground does tipple healths apace
When storms do fall, and shall not we?
A sorrow dares not shew its face,
When we are ships and sack 's the sea.   [1 *st.*

We do not suffer here alone;
Though we are beggar'd, so 's the King;
'Tis sin t' have wealth when he has none;
Tush! poverty 's a Royal thing!
When we are larded well with drink
Our heads shall turn as Round as theirs,
Our feet shall rise, our bodies sink
Clean down the wind, like Cavaliers.   [1 *st.*

Alexander Brome.

TO KEEP A TRUE LENT.

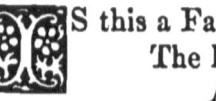S this a Fast, to keep
The larder lean?
And clean
From fat of veals, and sheep?

Is it to quit the dish
　　Of flesh, yet still
　　　　To fill
The platter high with fish ?

Is it to fast an hour,
　　Or ragg'd to go,
　　　　Or show
A downcast look, and sour?

No : 'tis a Fast, to dole
　　Thy sheaf of wheat,
　　　　And meat,
Unto the hungry soul.

It is to fast from strife,
　　From old debate,
　　　　And hate ;
To circumcise thy life.

To show a heart grief-rent ;
　　To starve thy sin,
　　　　Not bin ;
And that's to keep thy Lent.

Robert Herrick.

WHEN THE KING ENJOYS HIS OWN AGAIN.

WHAT Booker doth prognosticate,
　　Concerning kings' or kingdoms' fate ?
　　I think myself to be as wise
As he that gazeth on the skies :
　　My skill goes beyond
　　The depth of a Pond,

Or Rivers in the greatest rain;
        Thereby I can tell
        All things will be well
When the King enjoys his own again.

There's neither Swallow, Dove, nor Dade,
Can soar more high, nor deeper wade;
Nor show a reason from the stars
What causeth peace or civil wars:
        The Man in the Moon
        May wear out his shoon,
By running after Charles his wain;
        But all's to no end,
        For the times will not mend
Till the King enjoys his own again.

Though for a time we see Whitehall
With cobwebs hanging on the wall
Instead of silk and silver brave,
Which formerly it used to have,
        With rich perfume
        In every room,
Delightful to that princely train,
        Which again you shall see
        When the time it shall be
That the King enjoys his own again.

Full forty years the royal crown
Hath been his father's and his own;
And is there any one but he
That in the same should sharer be?
        For who better may
        The sceptre sway
Than he that hath such right to reign?
Then let's hope for a peace,
        For the wars will not cease
Till the King enjoys his own again.   [*1 st.*

Till then upon Ararat's hill
My hope shall cast her anchor still,
Until I see some peaceful dove
Bring home the branch I dearly love;
    Then will I wait
    Till the waters abate,
Which now disturb my troubled brain,
    Else never rejoice
    Till I hear the voice
That the King enjoys his own again.

Martin Parker.

FROM AN ODE UPON AN HYPOCRITICAL NONCONFORMIST.

HE does not pray, but prosecute,
    As if he went to law, his suit;
    Summons his Maker to appear
And answer what he shall prefer;
Returns him back his Gift of Prayer,
Not to petition, but declare;
    Exhibits cross complaints
Against him for the Breach of Covenants,
    And all the Charters of the Saints;
Pleads guilty to the Action, and yet stands
    Upon high terms and bold demands;
    Excepts against him and his laws,
And will be judge himself in his own cause;
    And grows more saucy and severe
Than th' heathen emperor was to Jupiter,
That used to wrangle with him, and dispute;
    And sometimes would speak softly in his ear
    And sometimes loud, and rant, and tear,
And threaten, if he did not grant his suit.

But when his painful Gifts he employs
In holding-forth, the virtue lies
Not in the letter of the sense,
But in the spiritual vehemence,
The power and dispensation of the voice,
The zealous pangs and agonies,
And heavenly turnings of the eyes;
The groans with which he piously destroys,
And draws the nonsense in the noise:
And grows so loud, as if he meant to force
And take in Heaven by violence ;
To fright the Saints into Salvation,
Or scare the Devil from Temptation ;
Until he falls so low and hoarse,
No kind of carnal sense
Can be made out of what he means:
But as the ancient Pagans were precise
To use no short-tail'd beast in sacrifice,
He still conforms to them, and has a care,
To allow the largest measure to his paltry ware.

Samuel Butler.

THE STORY OF PHŒBUS AND DAPHNE APPLIED.

HIRSIS, a youth of the inspired train,
Fair Sacharissa loved, but loved in vain :
Like Phœbus sung the no less am'rous boy,
Like Daphne she as lovely and as coy :
With numbers he the flying nymph pursues,
With numbers such as Phœbus self might use.
Such is the chase, when Love and Fancy leads,
O'er craggy mountains, and through flowery meads,
Invoked to testify the lover's care,
Or form some image of his cruel fair :

Urged with his fury like a wounded deer,
O'er these he fled, and now approaching near,
Had reach'd the nymph with his harmonious lay,
Whom all his charms could not incline to stay;
Yet what he sung in his immortal strain,
Though unsuccessful, was not sung in vain:
All but the nymph, that should redress his wrong,
Attend his passion, and approve his song.
Like Phœbus thus, acquiring unsought praise,
He catch'd at love, and fill'd his arm with bays.
Edmund Waller.

TO GOD, IN TIME OF PLUNDERING.

APINE has yet took nought from me:
But if it please my God I be
Brought at the last to th' utmost bit,
God make me thankful still for it.
I have been grateful for my store;
Let me say grace when there's no more.
Robert Herrick.

REST.

N with thy work, though thou beest hardly
prest;
Labour is held up by the hope of rest.
Robert Herrick.

THE CHARACTER OF AN ANTI-COVENANTER, OR MALIGNANT.

OULD you know these royal knaves,
Of free men would turn us slaves;
Who our union do defame
With rebellion's wicked name?

Read these verses, and ye 'll spring 'em,
Then on gibbets straight cause hing 'em.

They complain of sin and folly;
In these times so passing holy,
They their substance will not give,
Libertines that we may live.
Hold those subjects too, too wanton,
Under an old king dare canton.

Neglect they do our circ'lar tables,
Scorn our acts and laws as fables;
Of our battles talk but meekly,
With four sermons pleased are weekly;
Swear king Charles is neither papist,
Arminian, Lutheran, or atheist.

But that in his chamber-prayers,
Which are pour'd 'midst sighs and tears,
To avert God's fearful wrath,
Threat'ning us with blood and death;
Persuade they would the multitude,
This king too holy is and good.

They avouch we 'll weep and groan
When hundred kings we serve for one;
That each shire but blood affords,
To serve th' ambition of young lords;
Whose debts ere now had been redoubled,
If the state had not been troubled.

Slow they are our oath to swear,
Slower for it arms to bear:
They do concord love, and peace,
Would our enemies embrace,

Turn men proselytes by the word,
Not by musket, pike, and sword.

They swear that for religion's sake
We may not massacre, burn, sack :
That the beginning of these pleas,
Sprang from the ill-sped A B C's.
For servants that it is not well
Against their masters to rebel.

That that devotion is but slight,
Doth force men first to swear, then fight.
That our confession is indeed
Not the Apostolic Creed ;
Which of negations we contrive,
Which Turk and Jew may both subscrive.

That monies should men's daughters marry,
They on frantic war miscarry.
Whilst dear the soldiers they pay,
At last who will snatch all away,
And, as times turn worse and worse,
Catechise us by the purse.

That debts are paid with bold stern looks ;
That merchants pray on their 'compt books ;
That Justice dumb and sullen frowns,
To see in croslets hang'd her gowns ;
That preachers' ordinary theme
Is 'gainst monarchy to declaim.

That, since leagues we 'gan to swear,
Vice did ne'er so black appear ;
Oppression, bloodshed, ne'er more rife,
Foul jars between the man and wife:

I

Religion so contemn'd was never,
Whilst all are raging in a fever.

They tell by devils, and some sad chance,
That that detested league of France,
Which cost so many thousand lives,
And two kings, by religious knives,
Is amongst us, though few descry ;
Though they speak truth, yet say they lie.

He who says that night is night,
That cripple folk walk not upright,
That the owls into the spring
Do not nightingales out-sing,
That the seas we may not plough,
Ropes make of the rainy bow,
That the foxes keep not sheep,
That men waking do not sleep,
That all 's not gold doth gold appear—
Believe him not, although he swear.

To such syrens stop your ear,
Their societies forbear.
Ye may be tossed like a wave,
Verity may you deceive ;
Just fools they may make of you ;
Then hate them worse than Turk or Jew.

Were it not a dangerous thing,
Should we again obey the king ;
Lords lose should sovereignty,
Soldiers haste back to Germany ;
Justice should in our towns remain,
Poor men possess their own again ;
Brought out of hell that word of plunder,
More terrible than devil, or thunder,

Should with the covenant fly away,
And charity amongst us stay ;
Peace and plenty should us nourish,
True religion 'mongst us flourish ?

When you find these lying fellows,
Take and flower with them the gallows.
On others you may too lay hold,
In purse or chest, if they have gold.
Who wise or rich are in this nation,
Malignants are by protestation.

William Drummond.

A LYRIC TO MIRTH.

HILE the milder fates consent,
Let 's enjoy our merriment ;
Drink, and dance, and pipe, and play ;
Kiss our dollies night and day ;
Crown'd with clusters of the vine,
Let us sit and quaff our wine ;
Call on Bacchus, chaunt his praise ;
Shake the thyrse, and bite the bays ;
Rouse Anacreon from the dead,
And return him drunk to bed ;
Sing o'er Horace ; for ere long
Death will come and mar the song ;
Then shall Wilson and Gotiere
Never sing or play more here.

Robert Herrick.

TO THE VIRGINS, TO MAKE MUCH OF TIME.

GATHER ye rose-buds while ye may,
    Old Time is still a flying;
And this same flower that smiles to-day
To-morrow will be dying.

The glorious lamp of heaven, the sun,
    The higher he's a getting,
The sooner will his race be run,
    And nearer he's to setting.

That age is best, which is the first,
    When youth and blood are warmer;
But being spent, the worse and worst
    Times still succeed the former.

Then be not coy, but use your time,
    And while ye may, go marry;
For having lost but once your prime,
    You may for ever tarry.

                                    Robert Herrick.

TO A LADY SINGING A SONG OF HIS
COMPOSING.

CHLORIS, yourself you so excel
    When you vouchsafe to breathe my
        thought,
That like a spirit with this spell
    Of my own teaching I am caught.

The eagle's fate and mine are one,
　Which on the shaft that made him die
Espied a feather of his own,
　Wherewith he wont to soar so high.

Had Echo, with so sweet a grace,
　Narcissus' loud complaints return'd,
Not for reflection of his face,
　But of his voice, the boy had burn'd.
Edmund Waller.

ON A GIRDLE.

THAT which her slender waist confined,
　Shall now my joyful temples bind ;
　No monarch but would give his crown,
His arms might do what this has done.

It was my heaven's extremest sphere,
The pale which held that lovely deer ;
My joy, my grief, my hope, my love,
Did all within this circle move.

A narrow compass, and yet there
Dwelt all that 's good, and all that 's fair :
Give me but what this riband bound,
Take all the rest the sun goes round.
Edmund Waller.

TO LUCASTA.　FROM PRISON.

LONG in thy shackles, Liberty
　I ask not from these walls, but thee ;
　Left for awhile another's bride,
To fancy all the world beside.

Yet ere I do begin to love,
See, how I all my objects prove ;
Then my free soul to that confine,
'Twere possible I might call mine.

First I would be in love with Peace,
And her rich swelling breasts increase ;
But how, alas ! how may that be,
Despising Earth, she will love me ?

Fain would I be in love with War,
As my dear just avenging star ;
But War is loved so everywhere
Even he disdains a lodging here.

Thee and thy wounds I would bemoan,
Fair thorough-shot Religion ;
But he lives only that kills thee,
And who so binds thy hands, is free.

I would love a Parliament
As a main-prop from Heaven sent ;
But ah ! who's he, that would be wedded
To th' fairest body that 's beheaded ?

Next would I court my Liberty,
And then my birth-right, Property ;
But can that be, when it is known,
There 's nothing you can call your own ?

A Reformation I would have,
As for our griefs a Sovereign salve ;
That is, a cleansing of each wheel
Of state, that yet some rust doth feel.

But not a Reformation so,
As to reform were to o'erthrow ;
Like watches by unskilful men
Disjointed, and set ill again.

The Public Faith I would adore,
But she is bankrupt of her store;
Nor how to trust her can I see,
For she that cozens all, must me.

Since then none of these can be
Fit objects for my Love and me;
What then remains, but th' only spring
Of all our loves and joys? The KING.

He who, being the whole ball
Of day on earth, lends it to all;
When seeking to eclipse his right,
Blinded, we stand in our own light.

And now an universal mist
Of error is spread o'er each breast,
With such a fury edged, as is
Not found in th' inwards of th' abyss.

Oh, from thy glorious starry wain
Dispense on me one sacred beam
To light me where I soon may see
How to serve you, and you trust me!

Richard Lovelace.

THE POOR CAVALIER, IN MEMORY OF
HIS OLD SUIT.

THOUGH thou hast lasted 'bove a thousand days,
Till thou art aged and grey through adverse ways;
Yet malice in its highest dare pronounce
No other, but that thou wert scarlet once;
As in fair beauties innocently dead,
Their very paleness hath a tinct of red.

Under thy grey discernibly thin stream
Lies, like to shipwreck strawberries in cream.
I know 'tis vain to boast what thou hast been,
Yet thou wert red, when bloody votes were green ;
Ere ripe rebellion had a full-age power
To commit Laud and Gourney to the Tower ;
Ere middle-sighted judgment understood
That 'twas 'gainst sense o' th' Houses to be good.
It is no humble honour of thy fate
To follow in thy sufferings those of state.
I have observed since Leslie's coming in
Thou hast been still declining with the king,
Spite Fairfax and the Scots did all agree
To take our sleep from us, thy nap from thee.
But to declare thee in the State concern'd,
When Pomfret was relieved, then thou wert turn'd.
Prove thou didst wear new buttons on thy breast
When baffled Waller did retreat from th' West.
When taken Leicester raised our thoughts and speech,
Then thou wert reinforced in the breech.
Thanks to my tops and care which thought it meet
To rob my legs to keep thee on thy feet.
Nay, may I want belief if, when the report
Of lost Bridgewater first arrived at court,
Each whisper did not rend thee : I could tell
Still by new holes how our disasters fell.
At Langport, when the west was well ago
(A sad mischance) thy rear miscarried too,
And by a strong intelligence, the same time,
Thy hooks and buttons sprung with Sherburn's mine.
Now peace be with thy dust, whilst I do mourn
And, loyally industrious, close thy urn ;
For the next motion to a calm in th' air
Will thy poor extants into pieces tear :

And, as the wind when the wing'd nation pays
Their feather'd tribute, send it several ways;
One fragment would into Bridgewater fall,
In Sherburn one, in several garrisons all,
And th' insolent rebels at that sight be won
To think our thread of life like thine be done.
No, quondam suit, I'll keep thee from their claws,
Rotten as th' art, thou shalt be sound for th' cause.
Rather than to our prejudice be dispersed,
Thou shalt make Jack-o'-lents and Babies first,
Bait fishes' hooks to cozen mack'rels' lips,
Because they keep the seas with rebels' ships:
Make good a field of peas against jackdaw,
Reduce revolting turkeys into awe;
And every part of thee shall be employ'd
To serve against rebellion and pride.
And as the pious ancients used to rear
Tombs to the bodies which they know not where
To find, to thee, pure Shade of Shades (for in
This mortal life no ghost could be more thin)
This monumental paper I do vow,
And thank God I've another habit now.

John Cleveland.

MAJESTY IN MISERY.

An Imploration to the King of Kings.

(*Carisbrook*, 1648.)

GREAT monarch of the world, from whose power
    springs
     The potency and power of kings,
Record the royal woe my suffering sings;

And teach my tongue, that ever did confine
Its faculties in truth's seraphic line,
To track the treasons of thy foes and mine.

Nature and law, by thy divine decree,
(The only root of righteous royalty,)
With this dim diadem invested me:

With it, the sacred sceptre, purple robe,
The holy unction, and the royal globe:
Yet am I levell'd with the life of Job.

The fiercest furies, that do daily tread
Upon my grief, my grey discrowned head,
Are those that owe my bounty for their bread.

They raise a war, and christen it the cause,
Whilst sacrilegious hands have best applause,
Plunder and murder are the kingdom's laws;

Tyranny bears the title of taxation,
Revenge and robbery are reformation,
Oppression gains the name of sequestration.

My loyal subjects who in this bad season
Attend me (by the law of God and reason)
They dare impeach, and punish for high treason.

Next at the clergy do their furies frown,
Pious episcopacy must go down,
They will destroy the crozier and the crown.

Churchmen are chain'd, and schismatics are freed,
Mechanics preach, and holy fathers bleed,
The crown is crucified with the creed.

The church of England doth all faction foster,
The pulpit is usurp'd by each impostor,
Ex tempore excludes the *pater noster*.

The presbyter and independent seed
Springs with broad blades; to make religion bleed,
Herod and Pontius Pilate are agreed.

The corner stones misplaced by every pavier;
With such a bloody method and behaviour,
Their ancestors did crucify our Saviour.

My royal consort, from whose fruitful womb
So many princes legally have come,
Is forced in pilgrimage to seek a tomb.

Great Britain's heir is forced into France,
Whilst on his father's head his foes advance:
Poor child! he weeps out his inheritance.

With my own power my majesty they wound,
In the King's name the King himself's uncrown'd:
So doth the dust destroy the diamond.

With propositions daily they enchant
My people's ears, such as do reason daunt,
And the Almighty will not let me grant.

They promise to erect my royal stem,
To make me great, t' advance my diadem,
If I will first fall down and worship them!

But for refusal they devour my thrones,
Distress my children, and destroy my bones,
I fear they'll force me to make bread of stones.

My life they prize at such a slender rate,
That in my absence they draw bills of hate,
To prove the King a traitor to the State.

Felons obtain more privilege than I,
They are allow'd to answer ere they die;
'Tis death for me to ask the reason why.

But sacred Saviour, with thy words I woo
Thee to forgive, and not be bitter to
Such as thou know'st do not know what they do.

For since they from their Lord are so disjointed,
As to contemn those edicts he appointed,
How can they prize the power of his anointed?

Augment my patience, nullify my hate,
Preserve my issue, and inspire my mate;
Yet though we perish, bless this Church and State.

Charles the First.

A LENTEN LITANY.

*Composed for a confiding Brother, for the benefit and
edification of the faithful ones.*

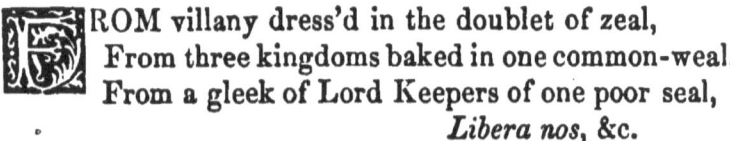ROM villany dress'd in the doublet of zeal,
From three kingdoms baked in one common-weal,
From a gleek of Lord Keepers of one poor seal,
Libera nos, &c.

From a preacher in buff, and a quarter-staff steeple, [4 *st.*
From th' unlimited sovereign power of the people,
From a kingdom that crawls on its knees like a cripple,
Libera nos, &c.

From a vinegar priest on a crab-tree stock,
From a foddering of prayer four hours by the clock,
From a holy sister with a pitiful smock,
>> *Libera nos,* &c.

From a hunger-starved sequestrator's maw,
From revelations and visions that never man saw,
From religion without either gospel or law,
>> *Libera nos,* &c.

From all that is said, and a thousand times more, [6 *st.*
From a Saint and his Charity to the poor,
From the Plagues that are kept for a Rebel in store,
>> *Libera nos,* &c.

The Second Part.

THAT if it please thee to assist
Our agitators and their list,
And hemp them with a gentle twist,
>> *Quæsumus te,* &c.

That it may please thee to suppose
Our actions are as good as those
That gull the people through the nose,
>> *Quæsumus te,* &c.

That it may please thee here to enter,
And fix the rumbling of our centre,
For we live all at Peradventure,
>> *Quæsumus te,* &c.

That it may please thee to unite
The flesh and bones unto the sprite,
Else, Faith and Literature, good-night, [9 *st.*
>> *Quæsumus te,* &c.
>>> *John Cleveland.*

THE KING BEHEADED.

CHARLES—ah, forbear, forbear! lest mortals prize
  His name too dearly, and idolatrize.
His name! our loss! Thrice cursed and forlorn
Be that black night which usher'd in this morn.

Charles, our dread sovereign!—hold! lest outlaw'd sense
Bribe and seduce tame reason to dispense
With those celestial powers; and distrust
Heaven can behold such treason, and prove just.

Charles our dread sovereign's murther'd! tremble! and
View what convulsions shoulder-shake this land,
Court, city, country, nay, three kingdoms run
To their last stage, and set with him their sun.

Charles our dread sovereign's murther'd at his gate!
Fell fiends! dire hydras of a stiff-neck'd state!
Strange body-politic! whose members spread,
And, monster-like, swell bigger than their Head.

Charles of Great Britain! He! who was the known
King of three realms, lies murther'd in his own.
He! he! who lived, and Faith's defender stood,
Died here to re-baptize it in his blood.

No more, no more. Fame's trump shall echo all
The rest in dreadful thunder. Such a fall
Great Christendom ne'er pattern'd; and 'twas strange
Earth's centre reel'd not at this dismal change.

The blow struck Britain blind, each well-set limb
By dislocation was lopt off in Him.
And though she yet lives, she lives but to condole
Three bleeding bodies left without a soul.

Religion puts on black, sad loyalty
Blushes, and mourns to see bright majesty
Butcher'd by such assassinates; nay, both
'Gainst God, 'gainst law, allegiance, and their oath.

Farewell, sad isle, farewell! Thy fatal glory
Is summ'd, cast up, and cancell'd in this story.

John Cleveland.

PSALM LXXXII.

OD sits upon the Throne of Kings,
And judges unto judgment brings :
   Why then so long
   Maintain you wrong
And favour lawless things ?

Defend the poor, the fatherless ;
Their crying injuries redress :
   And vindicate
   The desolate,
Whom wicked men oppress.

For they of knowledge have no light,
Nor will to know; but walk in night.
   Earth's bases fail ;
   No laws prevail;
Scarce one in heart upright.

Though gods, and sons of the Most High,
Yet you, like common men, shall die ;
   Like princes fall.
   Great God, judge all
The Earth, thy Monarchy.

George Sandys.

A MOCK SONG.

NOW Whitehall's in the grave,
        And our head is our slave,
    The bright pearl in his close shell of oyster;
        Now the mitre is lost,
        The proud prelates, too, cross'd,
And all Rome's confined to a cloister.
    He, that Tarquin was styled,
        Our white land's exiled,
            Yea, undefiled;
Not a court ape 's left to confute us;
        Then let your voices rise high,
        As your colours did fly,
            And flourishing cry:
Long live the brave Oliver Brutus.

        Now the sun is unarm'd,
        And the moon by us charm'd,
    All the stars dissolved to a jelly;
        Now the thighs of the Crown
        And the arms are lopp'd down,
And the body is all but a belly.
    Let the Commons go on,
        The town is our own,
            We'll rule alone:
For the knights have yielded their spent-gorge;
        And an order is ta'en
        With Honi Soit profane,
            Shout forth amain:
For our Dragon hath vanquish'd the St. George.

                        Richard Lovelace.

CAVALIER AND PURITAN SONG.

PART II.

WITH THE COMMONS.

K

A crown,
Golden in show, is but a wreath of thorns,
Brings dangers, troubles, cares, and sleepless nights,
To him who wears the regal diadem,
When on his shoulders each man's burden lies;
For therein stands the office of a King,
His honour, virtue, merit, and chief praise,
That for the Publick all this weight he bears.
Yet he, who reigns within himself, and rules
Passions, desires, and fears, is more a king;
Which every wise and virtuous man attains;
And who attains not, ill aspires to rule
Cities of men, or headstrong multitudes.

JOHN MILTON.

A DIALOGUE BETWEEN THE RESOLVED SOUL,

AND CREATED PLEASURE.

OURAGE, my soul! now learn to wield
The weight of thine immortal shield.
Close on thy head thy helmet bright;
Balance thy sword against the fight;
See where an army, strong as fair,
With silken banners spread the air.
Now, if thou be'st that thing divine,
In this day's combat let it shine,
And show that nature wants an art
To conquer one resolved heart.

PLEASURE.

Welcome, the creation's guest,
Lord of earth, and heaven's heir;
Lay aside that warlike crest,
And of nature's banquet share:
Where the souls of fruits and flowers,
Stand prepared to heighten yours.

SOUL.

I sup above, and cannot stay,
To bait so long upon the way.

PLEASURE.

On these downy pillows lie,
Whose soft plumes will thither fly :
On these roses, strewed so plain
Lest one leaf thy side should strain.

SOUL.

My gentler rest is on a thought,
Conscious of doing what I ought.

PLEASURE.

If thou be'st with perfumes pleased,
Such as oft the gods appeased,
Thou in fragrant clouds shalt show,
Like another god below.

SOUL.

A soul that knows not to presume,
Is heaven's, and its own, perfume.

PLEASURE.

Every thing doth seem to vie
Which should first attract thine eye :
But since none deserves that grace,
In this crystal view thy face.

SOUL.

When the Creator's skill is prized,
The rest is all but earth disguised.

PLEASURE.

Hark, how music then prepares
For thy stay these charming airs ;
Which the posting winds recall,
And suspend the river's fall.

SOUL.

Had I but any time to lose,
On this I would it all dispose.
Cease tempter! None can chain a mind,
Whom this sweet cordage cannot bind.

CHORUS.

Earth cannot show so brave a sight,
As when a single soul does fence
The battery of alluring sense,
And Heaven views it with delight.
  Then persevere; for still new charges sound:
  And if thou overcom'st, thou shalt be crown'd.

PLEASURE.

All that's costly, fair, and sweet,
  Which scatteringly doth shine,
Shall within one beauty meet,
  And she be only thine.

SOUL.

If things of sight such heavens be,
What heavens are those we cannot see?

PLEASURE.

Wheresoe'er thy foot shall go
  The minted gold shall lie;
Till thou purchase all below,
  And want new worlds to buy.

SOUL.

Wer't not for price who'd value gold?
And that's worth nought that can be sold.

PLEASURE.

Wilt thou all the glory have
    That war or peace commend ?
Half the world shall be thy slave,
    The other half thy friend.

SOUL.

What friends, if to myself untrue ?
What slaves, unless I captive you ?

PLEASURE.

Thou shalt know each hidden cause,
    And see the future time :
Try what depth the centre draws ;
    And then to heaven climb.

SOUL.

None thither mounts by the degree
Of knowledge, but humility.

CHORUS.

Triumph, triumph, victorious soul ;
    The world has not one pleasure more :
The rest does lie beyond the pole,
    And is thine everlasting store.

                                        Andrew Marvell.

FROM EURIPIDES.

THIS is true liberty, when freeborn men,
    Having to advise the public may speak free :
    Which he who can and will, deserves high praise ;
Who neither can nor will, may hold his peace :
What can be juster in a state than this ?   *John Milton.*

LABOUR IN VAIN.

HENCE away, you syrens, leave me,
   And unclasp your wanton arms,
   Sugar'd words shall ne'er deceive me,
Though you prove a thousand charms.
Fie, fie, forbear! no common snare
   Can ever my affection chain,
Your painted baits and poor deceits
   Are all bestow'd on me in vain.

I'm no slave to such as you be,
   Neither shall a snowy breast,
Wanton eye, or lip of ruby
   Ever rob me of my rest.
Go, go, display your beauty's ray,
   To some o'er soon enamour'd swain,
Those common wiles of sighs and smiles
   Are all bestow'd on me in vain.

I have elsewhere vow'd a duty;
   Turn away thy tempting eyes,
Show not me a naked beauty,
   Those impostures I despise.
My spirit loathes where gaudy clothes,
   And feigned oaths may love obtain;
I love Her so whose look swears No,
   That all your labours will be vain.

Can he prize the tainted posies
   Which on every breast are worn,
That may pluck the spotless roses
   From their never-touchèd thorn?

I can go rest on her sweet breast,
    That is the pride of Cynthia's train ;
Then hold your tongues ; your mermaid's songs
    Are all bestow'd on me in vain.

He's a fool that basely dallies,
    Where each peasant mates with him ;
Shall I haunt the thronged vallies,
    Whilst there's noble hills to climb ?
No, no ; though clowns are scared with frowns,
    I know the best can but disdain,
Then those I'll prove ; so shall your love,
    Be all bestowed on me in vain.   [2 st.

Proud she seem'd in the beginning,
    And disdain'd my looking on :
But that coy one in the winning,
    Proves a true one, being won.
Whate'er betide, she'll ne'er divide
    The favour she to me shall deign ;
But your fond love will fickle prove,
    And all that trust in you are vain.   [1 st.

Leave me, then, you syrens, leave me,
    Seek no more to work my harms ;
Crafty wiles cannot deceive me,
    Who am proof against your charms.
You labour may to lead astray
    The heart that constant shall remain :
And I the while will sit and smile,
    To see you spend your love in vain.

                      George Wither.

AT A SOLEMN MUSIC.

BLEST pair of Syrens, pledges of Heaven's joy,
    Sphere-born harmonious sisters, Voice and
        Verse,
Wed your divine sounds, and mixed power employ
Dead things with inbreathed sense able to pierce,
And to our high-raised fantasy present
That undisturbed song of pure consent,
Aye sung before the sapphire-colour'd throne
To Him that sits thereon,
With saintly shout and solemn jubilee ;
Where the bright Seraphim in burning row
Their loud uplifted angel-trumpets blow,
And the cherubic host in thousand quires
Touch their immortal harps of golden wires,
With those just spirits that wear victorious palms,
Hymns devout and holy psalms
Singing everlastingly :
That we on Earth with undiscording voice
May rightly answer that melodious noise ;
As once we did, till disproportion'd sin
Jarr'd against nature's chime, and with harsh din
Broke the fair music that all creatures made
To their great Lord, whose love their motion sway'd
In perfect diapason, whilst they stood
In first obedience, and their state of good.
Oh! may we soon again renew that Song,
And keep in tune with Heaven, till God ere long
To his celestial consort us unite,
To live with Him, and sing in endless morn of light !

                              John Milton.

THE POET.

Y art a poet is not made,
  For though by art some better'd be,
  Immediately his gift he had
From Thee, O God! from none but Thee:
And fitted in the womb he was
To be, by what Thou didst inspire,
In extraordinary place,
A chaplain of this lower choir;
  Most poets future things declare,
  And prophets, true or false, they are. [2 *st.*

But where this gift puffs up with pride,
The devil enters in thereby;
And through the same doth means provide
To raise his own inventions high:
Blasphemous fancies are infused,
All holy new things are expell'd;
He that hath most profanely mused,
Is famed as having most excell'd;
  And those are priests and prophets made
  To Him from whom their strains they had.

Such were those poets who of old
To heathen gods their hymns did frame,
Or have blasphemous fables told,
To truth's abuse and virtue's blame:
Such are these poets in these days,
Who vent the fumes of lust and wine,
Then crown each other's heads with bays,
As if their poems were divine;

And such, though they some truths foresee,
False-hearted and false prophets be.

Therefore since I reputed am
Among these few on whom the times
Imposed have a poet's name,
Lord, give me grace to shun their crimes.
My precious gift let me employ,
Not as imprudent poets use,
That grace and virtue to destroy
Which I should strengthen by my muse ;
    But help to free them of the wrongs
    Sustain'd by drunkards' rhymes and songs. [1 *st*.
                    George Wither.

BERMUDAS.

HERE the remote Bermudas ride,
    In the ocean's bosom unespied ;
      From a small boat, that row'd along,
The listening winds received this song.

  "What should we do but sing His praise,
That led us through the watery maze,
Unto an isle so long unknown,
And yet far kinder than our own ?
Where he the huge sea-monsters wracks,
That lift the deep upon their backs,
He lands us on a grassy stage,
Safe from the storms, and prelate's rage.
He gave us this eternal spring,
Which here enamels every thing ;
And sends the fowls to us in care,
On daily visits through the air.

He hangs in shades the orange bright,
Like, golden lamps in a green night,
And does in the pomegranates close,
Jewels more rich than Ormus shows ;
He makes the figs our mouths to meet,
And throws the melons at our feet,
But apples plants of such a price,
No tree could ever bear them twice ;
With cedars chosen by his hand,
From Lebanon, he stores the land,
And makes the hollow seas, that roar,
Proclaim the ambergris on shore.
He cast (of which we rather boast)
The gospel's pearl upon our coast;
And in these rocks for us did frame
A temple where to sound his name.
Oh ! let our voice his praise exalt,
Till it arrive at heaven's vault,
Which then, perhaps, rebounding, may
Echo beyond the Mexique Bay."

Thus sung they, in the English boat,
A holy and a cheerful note ;
And all the way, to guide their chime,
With falling oars they kept the time.

Andrew Marvell.

FROM SENECA.

There can be slain
No sacrifice to God more acceptable
Than an unjust and wicked King.

John Milton.

FROM WITHER'S MOTTO.

(Nec habeo, nec careo, nec curo.)

HAVE no pleasure in acquaintance where
The rules of state and ceremony are
Observed so seriously, that I must dance
And act o'er all the compliments of France
And Spain and Italy before I can
Be taken for a well-bred Englishman ;
And every time we meet, be forced again
To put in action that most idle scene.
'Mong these, much precious time (unto my cost)
And much true, hearty meaning have I lost.
Which having found, I do resolve therefore
To lose my Time and Friendship so no more.
I have no Muses that will serve the turn
At every triumph, and rejoice or mourn
Upon a minute's warning for their hire,   ·
If with old sherry they themselves inspire.
I am not of a temper like to those
That can provide an hour's sad talk in prose
For any funeral, and then go dine,
And choke my grief with sugar-plums and wine.
I cannot at the claret sit and laugh,
And then, half tipsy, write an epitaph.
I cannot (for my life) my pen compel
Upon the praise of any man to dwell,
Unless I know, or think, at least, his worth
To be the same which I have blazed forth.
Had I some honest suit, the gain of which
Would make me noble, eminent, and rich,
And that to compass it no means there were,
Unless I basely flatter'd some great peer ;

Would with that suit my ruin I might get,
If on those terms I would endeavour it.
I have no friends, that once affected were,
But to my heart this day they sit as near
As when I most endeared them, though they seem
To fall from my opinion or esteem;
For precious time in idle would be spent,
If I with all should always compliment;
And till my love I may to purpose show,
I care not whe'r they think I love or no:
For sure I am, if any find me changed,
Their greatness, not their meanness, me estranged.
I have not been ashamed to confess
My lowest fortunes, or the kindnesses
Of poorest men; nor have I proud been made
By any favour from a great man had.
I have not fear'd who my religion knows;
Nor ever for preferment made I shows
Of what I was not.   For, although I may
Through want be forced to put on worse array
Upon my body, I will ever find
Means to maintain a habit for my mind
Of truth in grain: and wear it in the sight
Of all the world, in all the world's despite.
What man is there among us doth not know
A thousand men this night to bed will go
Of many a hundred goodly things possest,
That shall have nought to-morrow but a chest,
And one poor sheet to lie in?   What I may
Next morning have, I know not; but to-day
A friend, meat, drink, and fitting clothes to wear,
Some books and papers which my jewels are,
A servant and a horse, all this I have,
And, when I die, one promised me a grave.

A grave, that quiet closet of content;
And I have built myself a monument.
But, as I live, excepting only this,
Which of my wealth the inventory is,
I have so little, I my oath might save,
If I should take it, that I nothing have.
    And yet what Want I? or who knoweth how
I may be richer made than I am now?
For as we see the smallest vials may
As full as greatest glasses be, though they
Much less contain, so my small portion gives
That full content to me in which he lives
Who most possesseth; and with larger store
I might fill others, but myself no more.
To what contents do men most wealthy mount
Which I enjoy not?   If their cares we count,
My clothing keeps me full as warm as their,
My meats unto my taste as pleasing are;
I feed enough my hunger to suffice;
I sleep till I myself am pleased to rise;
My dreams are sweet, and full of quiet be;
My waking cares as seldom trouble me.
I have as often times a sunny day,
And sport and laugh and sing as well as they;
I breathe as wholesome and as sweet an air,
As loving is my mistress, and as fair.
My body is as healthy, and I find
As little cause of sickness in my mind.
I am as wise, I think, as some of those;
And oft myself as foolishly dispose.
Yet I confess, in this my pilgrimage,
I like some infant am of tender age.
For as the child who from his father hath
Strayed in some grove, through many a crooked path,

Is sometime hopeful that he finds the way,
And sometime doubtful he runs more astray ;
Sometime with fair and easy paths doth meet,
Sometime with rougher tracts that stay his feet ;
Here runs, there goes, and yon amazed stays,
Now cries, and straight forgets his care and plays ;
Then, hearing where his loving Father calls,
Makes haste, but, through a zeal ill-guided, falls ;
Or runs some other way, until that He
(Whose love is more than his endeavours be)
To seek the wanderer forth, Himself doth come,
And take him in His arms, and bear him home.
So in this life, this grove of ignorance,
As to my homeward I myself advance,
Sometime aright, and sometime wrong I go,   .
Sometime my pace is speedy, sometime slow ;
Sometime I stagger, and sometime I fall ;
Sometime I sing, sometime for help I call.
One while my ways are pleasant unto me,
Another while, as full of cares they be :   .
Now I have courage, and do nothing fear ;
Anon, my spirits half-dejected are.
I doubt, and hope, and doubt, and hope again,
And many a change of passions I sustain,
In this my journey : so that now and then,
I lost may seem perhaps to other men.
But, whatsoe'er betide, I know full well,
My Father who above the clouds doth dwell,
An eye upon his wandering child doth cast,
And He will fetch me to my home at last.

   Then to vouchsafe me yet more favours here,
He that supplies my want hath took my Care.
A rush I care not who condemneth me,
That sees not what my soul's intentions be.

I care not though to all men known it were,
Both whom I love, or hate; for none I fear.
I care for no more time than will amount
To do my work and make up my account.
I care for no more money than will pay
The reckoning and the charges of the day;
And if I need not now, I will not borrow,
For fear of wants that I may have to-morrow.
My mind's my kingdom, and I will permit
No other's will to have the rule of it.
For I am free; and no man's power, I know,
Did make me thus, nor shall unmake me now.
But, through a spirit none can quench in me,
This Mind I got, and this my Mind shall be.

George Wither.

THE MANLY HEART.

SHALL I, wasting in despair,
  Die because a woman's fair?
    Or make pale my cheeks with care,
'Cause another's rosy are?
Be she fairer than the day,
Or the flowery meads in May,
If she be not so to me,
What care I how fair she be!

Should my heart be grieved or pined
'Cause I see a woman kind?
Or a well-disposed nature
Join'd with a lovely feature?
Be she meeker, kinder than
Turtle-dove or pelican;
If she be not so to me,
What care I how kind she be!

L

Shall a woman's virtues move
Me to perish for her love?
Or her well-deserving known
Make me quite forget mine own?
Be she with that goodness blest,
That may gain her name of Best,
If she be not such to me,
What care I how good she be!

'Cause her fortune seems too high,
Shall I play the fool and die?
Those that bear a noble mind,
Where they want of riches find,
Think what with them they would do
That without them dare to woo:
And unless that mind I see,
What care I, though great she be!

Great or good, or kind, or fair,
I will ne'er the more despair.
If she love me, this believe,
I will die ere she shall grieve.
If she slight me when I woo,
I can scorn and bid her go:
For if she be not for me,
What care I for whom she be!

George Wither.

MAN'S DAY AND NIGHT.

(*From Comus.*)

E that has light within his own clear breast
May sit i' th' centre, and enjoy bright day,
But he that hides a dark soul, and foul thoughts,
Benighted walks under the mid-day sun;
Himself is his own dungeon.   *John Milton.*

TO THE NIGHTINGALE.

NIGHTINGALE, that on yon bloomy spray
Warblest at eve, when all the woods are still,
   Thou with fresh hopes the Lover's heart dost
     fill,
While the jolly Hours lead on propitious May,
Thy liquid notes, that close the eye of Day,
  First heard before the shallow Cuckoo's bill,
  Portend success in love; Oh! if Jove's will
Have link'd that amorous power to thy soft lay,
Now timely sing, ere the rude Bird of Hate
  Foretell my hopeless doom, in some grove nigh:
As thou from year to year has sung too late
  For my relief; yet hadst no reason why,
Whether the Muse or Love call thee his mate,
  Both them I serve, and of their train am I.

John Milton.

FROM COMUS.

BACCHUS, that first from out the purple grape
   Crush'd the sweet poison of misused wine,
   After the Tuscan mariners transform'd,
Coasting the Tyrrhene shore, as the winds listed,
On Circè's island fell—who knows not Circè,
The daughter of the Sun? whose charmed cup
Whoever tasted lost his upright shape,
And downward fell into a grovelling swine—
This Nymph that gazed upon his clustering locks,
With ivy-berries wreathed, and his blithe youth,
Had by him, ere he parted thence, a Son

Much like his Father, but his Mother more,
Whom therefore she brought up, and Comus named.
Who ripe, and frolic of his full-grown age,
Roving the Celtic and Iberian fields,
At last betakes him to this ominous wood,
And, in thick shelter of black shades embower'd,
Excels his mother at her mighty art ;
Offering to every weary traveller
His orient liquor in a crystal glass,
To quench the drought of Phœbus; which as they taste
(For most do taste through fond intemperate thirst)
Soon as the Potion works, their human countenance,
The express resemblance of the gods, is changed
Into some brutish form of wolf, or bear,
Or ounce, or tiger, hog, or bearded goat,
All other parts remaining as they were,
And they, so perfect is their misery,
Not once perceive their foul disfigurement,
But boast themselves more comely than before ;
And all their friends and native home forget,
To roll with pleasure in a sensual sty.

Comus *enters with a Charming-Rod in one hand, his Glass*
  in the other ; with him a rout of monsters, headed like
  sundry sorts of wild beasts, but otherwise like men and
  women, their apparel glistering ; they come in making a
  riotous and unruly noise, with torches in their hands.

Com. The star that bids the shepherd fold
      Now the top of heaven doth hold,
      And the gilded car of day
      His glowing axle doth allay
      In the steep Atlantic stream,
      And the slope sun his upward beam

Shoots against the dusky pole,
Pacing toward the other goal
Of his chamber in the east.
Meanwhile welcome joy and feast,
Midnight shout and revelry,
Tipsy dance and jollity.
Braid your locks with rosy twine,
Dropping odours, dropping wine.
Rigour now is gone to bed,
And Advice, with scrupulous head,
Strict Age, and sour Severity,
With their grave saws, in slumber lie.
We, that are of purer fire,
Imitate the starry quire,
Who, in their nightly watchful spheres,
Lead in swift round the months and years.
The sounds and seas, with all their finny drove,
Now to the moon in wavering morrice move;
And, on the tawny sands and shelves,
Trip the pert fairies and the dapper elves.
By dimpled brook and fountain-brim,
The Wood-nymphs, deck'd with daisies trim,
Their merry wakes and pastimes keep :
What hath night to do with sleep ?
Night hath better sweets to prove,
Venus now wakes, and wakens Love.
Come, let us our rites begin,
'Tis only daylight that makes sin,
Which these dun shades will ne'er report.
   Hail goddess of nocturnal sport,
Dark-veil'd Cotytto, t' whom the secret flame
Of mid-night torches burns ; mysterious dame,
That ne'er art call'd but when the dragon-womb
Of Stygian darkness spets her thickest gloom,

And makes one blot of all the air,
Stay thy cloudy ebon chair,
Wherein thou ridest with Hecat', and befriend
Us thy vow'd priests, till utmost end
Of all thy dues be done, and none left out;
Ere the blabbing eastern scout,
The nice Morn on the Indian steep
From her cabin'd loophole peep,
And to the tell-tale Sun descry
Our conceal'd solemnity.
Come, knit hands, and beat the ground
In a light fantastic round.

John Milton.

FROM BRITAIN'S REMEMBRANCER.

To the King. (1628.)

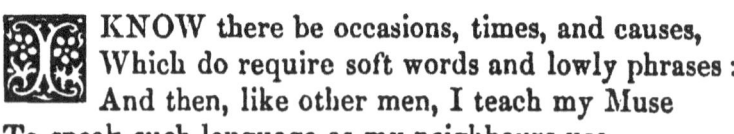 KNOW there be occasions, times, and causes,
Which do require soft words and lowly phrases :
And then, like other men, I teach my Muse
To speak such language as my neighbours use.

But there are also times which will require
That we should with our numbers mingle fire:
And then I vent bold words that you and they
Who come to hear them, take occasion may
To ask or to examine, what's the matter,
My verse speaks tartly when most writers flatter.
For, by that means, you may experienced grow
In many things which else you should not know.

My lines are loyal, though they bold appear ;
And though at first they make some readers fear

I want good manners, yet, when they are weigh'd,
It will be found that I have nothing said,
In manner or in matter, worthy blame,
If they alone shall judge me for the same
Who know true virtue's language ; and how free
From glozing terms her servants use to be.

I count not each man valiant who dares die,
Or venture on a mischief desperately,
When either heat of youth, or wine, or passion,
Shall whet him on before consideration ;
Nor will I any man a coward call,
Although I see him tremble and look pale
In dangerous attempts, unless he slack
His just resolves by basely stepping back.
Give me the man that with a quaking arm
Walks with a steadfast mind through greatest harm ;
And, though his flesh doth tremble, makes it stand
To execute what reason doth command.
Give me the soul that knowingly descries
All dangers, and all possibilities
Of outward perils, and yet doth persèvere
In every lawful action howsoever.
Give me that heart which in itself doth war
With many frailties (who like traitors are
In some besieged fort), and hath to do
With outward foes and inward terrors too ;
Yet of himself and them a conquest makes,
And still proceeds in what he undertakes.

My prince and country, though perhaps I be
Not much to them, are both most dear to me.
And may I perish if, to save my life,
I would betwixt that couple nourish strife.

I may, perchance, in what I best intend,
Have neither king nor people to my friend ;
Yet will I speak my mind to profit them,
Though both should, for my labour, me condemn.
Although we heed not, or else will not see
Those maladies which daily growing be,
I find (and I do much compassionate
What I behold) a rupture in the State
Of this great body. .   .   .   ·

Thou art this body, England, and thy head
Is our dread Sov'reign.   The distemper bred
Betwixt you two, from one of you doth flow,
And which it is I purpose here to show.
If in thy King, O Britain, aught amiss
Appears to be, 'twixt God and him it is.
Of Him he shall be judged.   What to thee
Pertaineth it his censurer to be ?
Thy general voice but newly did confess
In him much virtue and much hopefulness ;
And he so late assumed his diadem,
That there hath scarce been time enough for him
Those evils to perform that may infer
A general mischief.   Neither do I hear
Of ought, as yet, which thou to him canst lay
But that he doth to thee thy will deny,
Or, with a gentle stoutness, claim and strive
For what he thinks his just prerogative.
And why, I prithee, may not all this flow
From some corruptions which in thee do grow
Without his fault ?   Why may not, for thy crimes,
Some instrument of Satan, in these times,
Be suffer'd to obscure from him a while
The truth of things, and his belief beguile

With virtuous shows, discreet and good pretences,
To plague and punish thee for thy offences ?
Why may not God (and justly too) permit
Some sycophant, or cunning hypocrite,
For thy hypocrisies, to steal away
His heart from thee ?   And goodly colours lay
On projects which may cause him to undo thee,
And think that he no wrong hath done unto thee ?
Nay, wherefore may not some thy king advise,
To that which seems to wrong thy liberties,
Yet in themselves be honest men and just,
Who have abused been by those they trust ?
Thy wickedness deserves it; and that he,
Who in himself is good, should bring to thee
No profit by his goodness, but augment
Thy sorrows till thy follies thou repent ?
For what is in itself from evil free,
Is evil made to those that evil be.
Go cast yourselves before him with submission ;
Present him with petition on petition.
With one accord, and with a fearless face,
Inform him how much hindrance or disgrace,
Or danger to the land there may accrue,
If he your loyal counsel shall eschew.
For God, because his laws we disobey,
Us at our sovereign's feet doth mean to lay,
To humble us awhile.   If we repent,
To all our loyal suits he will assent.
If otherwise, God will give up this land,
Our lives and freedoms all into his hand.

George Wither.

THE FAIR SINGER.

TO make a final conquest of all me,
   Love did compose so sweet an enemy,
   In whom both beauties to my death agree,
Joining themselves in fatal harmony,
That, while she with her eyes my heart does bind,
She with her voice might captivate my mind.

I could have fled from one but singly fair ;
   My disentangled soul itself might save,
Breaking the curlèd trammels of her hair ;
   But how should I avoid to be her slave,
Whose subtle art invisibly can wreath
   My fetters of the very air I breathe ?

It had been easy fighting in some plain,
   Where victory might hang in equal choice ;
But all resistance against her is vain,
   Who has the advantage both of eyes and voice ;
And all my forces needs must be undone,
She having gainèd both the wind and sun.

                       Andrew Marvell.

SONG ON MAY MORNING.

NOW the bright Morning-Star, Day's harbinger,
   Comes dancing from the east, and leads with her
   The flowery May, who from her green lap throws
The yellow cowslip and the pale primrose.
   Hail, bounteous May, that dost inspire
   Mirth, and youth, and warm desire !

Woods and groves are of thy dressing,
Hill and dale doth boast thy blessing.
Thus we salute thee with our early song,
And welcome thee, and wish thee long.

John Milton.

MUSIC'S EMPIRE.

FIRST was the world as one great cymbal made,
Where jarring winds to infant nature play'd;
All music was a solitary sound,
To hollow rocks and murmuring fountains bound.
Jubal first made the wilder notes agree,
And Jubal tunèd Music's jubilee;
He call'd the echoes from their sullen cell,
And built the Organ's City, where they dwell;
Each sought a consort in that lovely place,
And virgin trebles wed the manly bass;
From whence the progeny of numbers new
Into harmonious colonies withdrew;
Some to the lute, some to the viol went,
And others chose the cornet eloquent;
These practising the wind, and those the wire,
To sing man's triumphs, or in heaven's choir.
Then Music, the mosaic of the air,
Did of all these a solemn noise prepare,
With which she gain'd the Empire of the ear,
Including all between the earth and sphere.
Victorious sounds! yet here your homage do
Unto a gentler conqueror than you;
Who, though he flies the music of his praise,
Would with you Heaven's Hallelujahs raise.

Andrew Marvell.

TO MR. H. LAWES, ON HIS AIRS.

ARRY, whose tuneful and well-measured song
 First taught our English music how to span
  Words with just note and accent, not to scan
 With Midas' ears, committing short and long,
Thy worth and skill exempts thee from the throng,
 With praise enough for envy to look wan;
 To after-age thou shalt be writ the man,
 That with smooth air could humour best our tongue.
Thou honourest verse, and verse must lend her wing
 To honour thee, the priest of Phœbus' quire,
 That tunest their happiest lines in hymn or story.
Dante shall give Fame leave to set thee higher
 Than his Casella, whom he woo'd to sing,
 Met in the milder shades of Purgatory.

       John Milton.

LIBERTY.

(*From a Sonnet.*)

H[EY] bawl for freedom in their senseless
  mood,
  And still revolt when truth would set them
  free.
 Licence they mean when they cry liberty;
For who loves that must first be wise and good;
 But from that mark how far they rove we see
For all this waste of wealth and loss of blood.

       John Milton.

WHEN THE ASSAULT WAS INTENDED TO
BRENTFORD.

CAPTAIN, or colonel, or knight in arms,
 Whose chance on these defenceless doors may
  seize,
If deed of honour did thee ever please,
Guard them, and him within protect from harms.
He can requite thee, for he knows the charms
 That call fame on such gentle acts as these;
 And he can spread thy name o'er lands and seas,
Whatever clime the sun's bright circle warms.
Lift not thy spear against the Muses' bower.
 The great Emathian conqueror bid spare
 The house of Pindarus, when temple and tower
Went to the ground; and the repeated air
 Of sad Electra's poet had the power
 To save the Athenian walls from ruin bare.

      John Milton.

THE SOLDIER.

NOW in myself I notice take,
 What life we soldiers lead,
 My hair stands up, my heart doth ache,
My soul is full of dread;
  And to declare
  This horrid fear,
Throughout my bones I feel
  A shiv'ring cold
  On me lay hold,
And run from head to heel.

It is not loss of limbs or breath
   Which hath me so dismay'd,
Nor mortal wounds, nor groans of death
   Have made me thus array'd :
      When cannons roar,
      I start no more
    Than mountains from their place,
      Nor feel I fears,
      Though swords and spears
    Are darted at my face.

A soldier it would ill become
   Such common things to fear,
The shouts of war, the thund'ring drum,
   His courage up doth cheer :
      Though dust and smoke
      His passage choke,
    He boldly marcheth on,
      And thinketh scorn
      His back to turn,
    Till all be lost or won.

The flashing fires, the whizzing shot,
   Distemper not his wits;
The barbed steed he dreadeth not,
   Nor him who thereon sits;
      But through the field,
      With sword and shield,
    He cutteth forth his way,
      And through a flood
      Of reeking blood,
    Wades on without dismay.

That whereupon the dread begins
   Which thus apalleth me,

Is that huge troop of crying sins
  Which rife in soldiers be;
    The wicked mind,
    Wherewith I find
  Into the field they go,
    More terror hath,
    Than all the wrath
  And engines of the foe.   [1 *st.*

Defend me, Lord! from those misdeeds
  Which my profession shame,
And from the vengeance that succeeds
  When we are so to blame:
      Preserve me far
      From acts of war,
    Where Thou dost peace command;
      And in my breast
      Let mercy rest,
    Though justice use my hand.   [2 *st.*

Be Thou my leader to the field,
  My head in battle arm;
Be Thou a breastplate and a shield,
  To keep my soul from harm;
      For live or die,
      I will rely
    On Thee, O Lord! alone;
      And in this trust,
      Though fall I must,
    I cannot be undone.

George Wither.

THE COLOURS TAKEN AT NASEBY.

(*June 14th*, 1645. *From Vox Pacifica.*)

HE scornful adversaries rushèd on,
 To policy and strength themselves commending,
 The Lord of Hosts our friends relied upon,
With prayers fighting, and with faith defending :
And lo, God gave their foes into their hand :
For when He fighteth, who can then withstand ?
The victory was great, and every one
 Observed what circumstances pleased him best ;
But that my thoughts did most insist upon,
 (Which others peradventure minded least,)
These loyal ensigns from the field were brought,
 The lion rampant and the dragon flying,
The roses and portcullis ; which methought
 Were pledges future mercy signifying.
And so, no doubt, they shall be, if that race
 To which God calleth us we now shall run ;
And better heed the tokens of this grace
 And earnests of His love than we have done ;
For valiant Fairfax now hath sent us home
In hieroglyphic, signs of things to come.

The ramping lion (which doth signify
 A raging tyrant) may an earnest be
That God will from oppressing tyranny
 Upon our good abearing set us free.
A dragon is that most prodigious beast
 Whereby the Holy Ghost hath typified
That foe by whom the saints are most opprest,
 And by whom daily they are crucified.

The taking of that ensign may foreshew
   That, if we faithfully the work endeavour,
The power of antichrist we shall subdue,
   And from these islands cast his throne for ever.
Vouchsafe us power, O God, vouchsafe us grace
   To drive him and his angels from this place.
The joining of the roses doth declare
   That God will to these honours us restore,
Wherewith he crown'd us when, in peace and war,
   We on our crest those lovely flowers wore.
Their blushing beauties are, to me, a sign
   Of that delightful and soul-pleasing grace
Which will make lovely our church discipline
   When God hath changed our discords into peace.
The sweetness and the virtues of the rose
   Do seem to promise to us those effects,
And fruit which from internal graces flows,
   Yea, and their prickles are, in some respects,
Significant, for I by them foresee
   That his corrections always needful be.
By taking their portcullis from the foe
   It may portend (and, if with penitence
We prosecute the work, it shall be so)
   That we have taken from them their defence.
It may betoken also that God's hand
   Will bar our gates and make our city strong,
And, by his mercy, fortify the land,
   Against all them who seek to do us wrong.
But, for a surer token of this grace,
   God sends us home, among the spoils of war,
That cabinet of mischief wherein was
   The proof of what our foes' intentions are :
And that their projects God will still disclose,
And fool their policies, this prize foreshows.

M   *George Wither.*

ON THE NEW FORCERS OF CONSCIENCE UNDER THE LONG PARLIAMENT.

BECAUSE you have thrown off your prelate-lord,
    And with stiff vows renounced his liturgy,
    To seize the widow'd whore Plurality
From them whose sin ye envied, not abhorr'd;
Dare ye for this adjure the civil sword
    To force our consciences that Christ set free,
    And ride us with a classic hierarchy,
    Taught ye by mere A. S. and Rotherford?
Men, whose life, learning, faith, and pure intent
    Would have been held in high esteem with Paul,
    Must now be named and printed heretics
By shallow Edwards and Scotch What-d'ye-call.
    But we do hope to find out all your tricks,
    Your plots and packing worse than those of Trent,
        That so the Parliament
May, with their wholesome and preventive shears,
Clip your phylacteries, though bauk your ears,
        And succour our just fears,
When they shall read this clearly in your charge,
New *presbyter* is but old *priest* writ large.

John Milton.

LABOUR AND CHEERFULNESS.

(*From a Sonnet.*)

TO measure life learn thou betimes, and know
    Toward solid good what leads the nearest way;
    For other things mild heaven a time ordains,
And disapproves that care, though wise in show,
    That with superfluous burdens loads the day,
    And when God sends a cheerful hour, refrains.

John Milton.

TO THE LORD GENERAL FAIRFAX.

AIRFAX, whose name in arms through Europe
 rings,
 Filling each mouth with envy or with praise,
And all her jealous monarchs with amaze
And rumours loud, that daunt remotest kings,
Thy firm unshaken virtue ever brings
 Victory home, though new rebellions raise
 Their hydra-heads, and the false North displays
 Her broken league to imp their serpent-wings.
Oh! yet a nobler task awaits thy hand . . .
 For what can war but endless war still breed
 Till truth and right from violence be freed,
And public faith clear'd from the shameful brand
 Of public fraud? In vain doth valour bleed,
 While avarice and rapine share the land.

John Milton.

THE CONQUERED KING.

(*From Prosopopoeia Britannica.* 1648.)

REALM that fears to call her trustee to
 Account for aught misdone, or left to do,
 Is like those children who do fear the shows
Which they themselves set up to scare the crows;
And they, who think you have no rightful power
To curb his fury who might you devour,
May think as well they should not put a clog,
Or hang a chain, upon a shepherd's dog,

Although he daily bites and kills the sheep,
Which he was only bred and fed to keep.
Men do not use to hunt a beast of prey,
To take him and then let him go away.
Kings who without control the sceptre sway'd
As tameless are as lions that have prey'd,
Which, howsoever you shall use or feed them,
Will soon grow dangerous unless you heed them.
When he whose ancient birthright was quite lost
Hath by expense of labour, time and cost,
A lawful repossession of it sought,
And at the law his suit to trial brought;
Obtain'd a verdict, judgment, execution,
And full possession without diminution,
What, for a friend! I pray, were such a one
Who should persuade this man when all were done,
To waive his lawful right so dearly bought,
To treat with him who his undoing sought,
And, uncompell'd, refer unto debate
What he should take or leave of that estate?

George Wither.

A HORATIAN ODE

Upon Cromwell's return from Ireland.

THE forward youth that would appear,
    Must now forsake his Muses dear,
        Nor in the shadows sing
        His numbers languishing:
'Tis time to leave the books in dust,
And oil the unused armour's rust,
        Removing from the wall
        The corselet of the hall.

So restless Cromwell could not cease
In the inglorious arts of peace,
  But through adventurous war
  Urged his active star ;
And, like the three-forked lightning, first
Breaking the clouds where it was nurst,
  Did thorough his own side
  His fiery way divide ;
(For 'tis all one to courage high,
The emulous, or enemy,
  And with such to inclose,
  Is more than to oppose ;)
Then burning through the air he went,
And palaces and temples rent ;
  And Cæsar's head at last
  Did through his laurels blast.
'Tis madness to resist or blame
The force of angry heaven's flame ;
  And if we would speak true,
  Much to the man is due,
Who from his private gardens, where
He lived reserved and austere,
  As if his highest plot
  To plant the bergamot,
Could by industrious valour climb
To ruin the great work of Time,
  And cast the kingdoms old,
  Into another mould.
Though Justice against Fate complain,
And plead the ancient rights in vain,
  (But those do hold or break,
  As men are strong or weak,)
Nature, that hateth emptiness,
Allows of penetration less,

And therefore must make room
Where greater spirits come.
What field of all the civil war,
Where his were not the deepest scar ?
    And Hampton shows what part
    He had of wiser art ;
Where, twining subtle fears with hope,
He wove a net of such a scope
    That Charles himself might chase
    To Carisbrook's narrow case,
That thence the royal actor borne,
The tragic scaffold might adorn,
    While round the armed bands,
    Did clap their bloody hands.
He nothing common did, or mean,
Upon that memorable scene,
    But with his keener eye
    The axe's edge did try ;
Nor call'd the gods with vulgar spite
To vindicate his helpless right,
    But bow'd his comely head
    Down, as upon a bed.
This was that memorable hour,
Which first assured the forcèd power ;
    So, when they did design
    The capitol's first line,
A bleeding head, where they begun,
Did fright the architects to run ;
    And yet in that the state
    Foresaw its happy fate.
And now the Irish are ashamed
To see themselves in one year tamed ;
    So much one man can do,
    That does both act and know.

They can affirm his praises best,
And have, though overcome, confess'd
    How good he is, how just,
    And fit for highest trust.
Nor yet grown stiffer with command,
But still in the republic's hand,
    (How fit he is to sway,
    That can so well obey!)
He to the Commons' feet presents
A kingdom for his first year's rents;
    And, what he may, forbears
    His fame, to make it theirs;
And has his sword and spoils ungirt,
To lay them at the public's skirt:
    So when the falcon high
    Falls heavy from the sky,
She, having kill'd, no more doth search
But on the next green bough to perch;
    Where, when he first does lure,
    The falconer has her sure.
What may not then our isle presume,
While victory his crest does plume?
    What may not others fear,
    If thus he crowns each year?
As Cæsar, he, ere long, to Gaul,
To Italy a Hannibal,
    And to all states not free,
    Shall climacteric be.
The Pict no shelter now shall find
Within his parti-colour'd mind,
    But, from this valour sad,
    Shrink underneath the plaid;
Happy, if in the tufted brake,
The English hunter him mistake,

    Nor lay his hounds in near
    The Caledonian deer.
But thou, the war's and fortune's son,
March indefatigably on,
        And for the last effect,
        Still keep the sword erect ;
Beside the force it has to fright
The spirits of the shady night,
        The same arts that did gain
        A power, must it maintain.

Andrew Marvell.

TO THE LORD GENERAL CROMWELL.

MAY 16, 1652.

*On the Proposals of certain Ministers of the Committee
for the Propagation of the Gospel.*

CROMWELL, our chief of men, who through a
        cloud
        Not of war only, but detractions rude,
Guided by faith and matchless fortitude,
  To peace and truth thy glorious way hast plough'd,
And on the neck of crownèd Fortune proud
    Hast rear'd God's trophies, and his work pursued,
    While Darwen stream with blood of Scots imbrued,
    And Dunbar field resounds thy praises loud,
And Worcester's laureate wreath.   Yet much remains
    To conquer still ; peace hath her victories
    No less renown'd than war : new foes arise
Threatening to bind our souls with secular chains.
    Help us to save free conscience from the paw
    Of hireling wolves, whose Gospel is their maw.

John Milton.

TO SIR HENRY VANE THE YOUNGER.

(1652 ?)

VANE, young in years, but in sage counsel old,
  Than whom a better senator ne'er held
  The helm of Rome, when gowns not arms repell'd
The fierce Epirot and the African bold ;
Whether to settle peace, or to unfold
  The drift of hollow states hard to be spell'd ;
  Then to advise how war may, best upheld,
  Move by her two main nerves, iron and gold,
In all her equipage ; besides to know
  Both spiritual power and civil, what each means,
  What severs each, thou hast learn'd, which few have
      done.
The bounds of either sword to thee we owe :
  Therefore on thy firm hand Religion leans
  In peace, and reckons thee her eldest son.

FROM " THE PROTECTOR."

(1655.)

THIS glorious title hath in it exprest,
  No stamp of self-selection like the rest,
  But marks forth one (as if from heaven sent
      down),
Who seeks his people's weal more than his own.
It is the chiefest of God's attributes,
Which he to these men whom he here deputes,
Communicates ; and ought therefore by none
To be assumed but God-like men alone,

Who in their hearts have purposed to be,
At least by imitation, such as He:
And ready to contribute, in His stead,
Due succours to all suppliants in their need.
It is a name of mercy and affection,
Which not alone engageth to protection,
But likewise to a strenuous opposition
Of tyrant's tyrannies and all oppression.
For to be called a Nation to protect
Implies (at least in some degree) the effect
Of every means which may be helpful to
Those works which God provided him to do ;
And nobler is, in that respect, than those
Loud-sounding titles which our fathers chose.

George Wither.

THE FIRST ANNIVERSARY OF THE GOVERNMEN

UNDER HIS ROYAL HIGHNESS THE

LORD PROTECTOR.

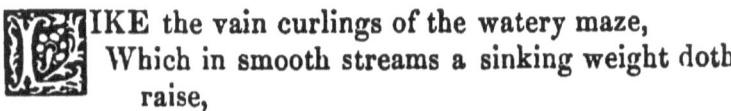IKE the vain curlings of the watery maze,
    Which in smooth streams a sinking weight doth
        raise,
So man, declining, always disappears
In the weak circles of increasing years ;
And his short tumults of themselves compose,
While flowing time above his head doth close.

   Cromwell alone, with greater vigour runs,
(Sun-like) the stages of succeeding suns,

And still the day which he doth next restore,
Is the just wonder of the day before ;
Cromwell alone doth with new lustre spring,
And shines the jewel of the yearly ring.
'Tis he the force of scatter'd time contracts,
And in one year the work of ages acts :
While heavy monarchs make a wide return,
Longer and more malignant than Saturn,
And they, though all Platonic years should reign,
In the same posture would be found again ;
Their earthly projects under ground they lay,
More slow and brittle than the China clay ;
Well may they strive to leave them on their son,
For one thing never was by one king done.
Yet some, more active, for a frontier town
Took in by proxy, begs a false renown ;
Another triumphs at the public cost,
And will have won, if he no more have lost ;
They fight by others, but in person wrong,
And only are against their subjects strong.   [48 *ll.*

   All other matters yield, and may be ruled,
But who the minds of stubborn men can build ?
No quarry bears a stone so hardly wrought,
Nor with such labour from its centre brought :
None to be sunk in the foundation bends,
Each in the house the highest place contends ;
And each the hand that lays him will direct,
And some fall back upon the architect ;
Yet all, composed by his attractive song,
Into the animated city throng.   [12 *ll.*

   When for his foot he thus a place had found,
He hurls e'er since the world about him round ;

And in his several aspects, like a star,
Here shines in peace, and thither shoots a war,
While by his beams observing princes steer,
And wisely court the influence they fear.   [12 *ll.*
Unhappy princes, ignorantly bred,
By malice some, by error more misled,
If gracious Heaven to my life give length,
Leisure to time, and to my weakness strength,
Then shall I once with graver accents shake
Your regal sloth and your long slumbers wake,
Like the shrill huntsman that prevents the east,
Winding his horn to kings that chase the beast!

Till then my muse shall halloo far behind
Angelic Cromwell, who outwings the wind,
And in dark nights, and in cold days, alone
Pursues the monster thorough every throne,
Which shrinking to her Roman den impure,
Gnashes her gory teeth; nor there secure.

Hence oft I think, if in some happy hour
High grace should meet in one with highest power,
And then a seasonable people still
Should bend to his, as he to Heaven's will,
What we might hope, what wonderful effect
From such a wish'd conjuncture might reflect!
Sure, the mysterious work, where none withstand,
Would forthwith finish under such a hand;
Foreshorten'd time its useless course would stay,
And soon precipitate the latest day;
But a thick cloud about that morning lies,
And intercepts the beam to mortal eyes,
That 'tis the most which we determine can,
If these the times, then this must be the man;

And well he therefore does, and well has guess'd,
Who in his age has always forward press'd
And knowing not where Heaven's choice may light,
Girds yet his sword, and ready stands to fight.   [10 *ll.*

    And thou, great Cromwell, for whose happy birth
A mould was chosen out of better earth,
Whose saint-like mother we did lately see
Live out an age, long as a pedigree,
That she might seem, could we the fall dispute,
To have smelt the blossom, and not eat the fruit,—
Though none does of more lasting parents grow,
Yet never any did them honour so.
Though thou thine heart from evil still sustain'd,
And always hast thy tongue from fraud refrain'd.
Thou, who so oft through storms of thundering lead
Hast borne securely thine undaunted head;
Thy breast through poniarding conspiracies,
Drawn from the sheath of lying prophecies,
The proof beyond all other force or skill,
Our sins endanger, and shall one day kill.
How near they fail'd, and in thy sudden fall,
At once assay'd to overturn us all!
Our British fury, struggling to be free,
Hurried thy horses, while they hurried thee;
When thou hadst almost quit thy mortal cares,
And soil'd in dust thy crown of silver hairs.   [10 *ll.*
    But the poor beasts, wanting their noble guide,
(What could they more?) shrunk guiltily aside:
First winged fear transports them far away,
And leaden sorrow then their flight did stay.
See how they both their towering crests abate,
And the green grass and their known mangers hate,
Nor through wide nostrils snuff the wanton air,

Nor their round hoofs or curled manes compare ;
With wandering eyes and restless ears they stood,
And with shrill neighings ask'd him of the wood. [14 *ll.*

But thee triumphant, hence, the fiery car
And fiery steeds had borne out of the war.   [4 *ll.*
For all delight of life thou then didst lose,
When to command thou didst thyself depose,
Resigning up thy privacy so dear,
To turn the headstrong people's charioteer ;
For to be Cromwell was a greater thing,
Than aught below, or yet above, a king :
Therefore thou rather didst thyself depress,
Yielding to rule, because it made thee less.

For neither didst thou from the first apply
Thy sober spirit unto things too high ;
But in thine own fields exercisedst long
A healthful mind within a body strong,
Till at the seventh time, thou in the skies,
As a small cloud, like a man's hand didst rise.   [4 *ll.*
What since thou didst, a higher force thee push'd
Still from behind, and it before thee rush'd.
Though undiscern'd among the tumult blind,
Who think those high decrees by man design'd,
'Twas Heaven would not that e'er thy power should
    cease,
But walk still middle betwixt war and peace ;
Choosing each stone, and poising every weight,
Trying the measures of the breadth and height,
Here pulling down, and there erecting new,
Founding a firm state by proportions true.

When Gideon so did from the war retreat,
Yet by the conquest of two kings grown great,
He on the peace extends a warlike power,

And Israel, silent, saw him rase the tower,
And how he Succoth's elders durst suppress
With thorns and briers of the wilderness ;
No king might ever such a force have done,
Yet would not he be lord, nor yet his son.

Thou with the same strength, and a heart so plain,
Didst like thine olive still refuse to reign ;
Though why should others all thy labour spoil,
And brambles be anointed with thine oil,
Whose climbing flame, without a timely stop,
Had quickly levell'd every cedar's top ?
Therefore, first growing to thyself a law,
The ambitious shrubs thou in just time didst awe.

So have I seen at sea, when whirling winds
Hurry the bark, but more the seamen's minds,
Who with mistaken course salute the sand,
And threatening rocks misapprehend for land,—
While baleful tritons to the shipwreck guide,
And corposants [1] along the tacklings slide,—
The passengers all wearied out before,
Giddy, and wishing for the fatal shore,—
Some lusty mate, who with more careful eye,
Counted the hours, and every star did spy,
The helm does from the artless steersman strain,
And doubles back unto the safer main :
What though awhile they grumble, discontent ?
Saving himself, he does their loss prevent.

'Tis not a freedom that, where all command,
Nor tyranny, where one does them withstand ;
But who of both the bounders knows to lay,
Him, as their father, must the state obey.

---

[1] Meteoric lights ; from Spanish, "cuerpo santo."

Thou and thy house, like Noah's eight did rest,
Left by the war's flood, on the mountain's crest;
And the large vale lay subject to thy will,
Which thou but as an husbandman, wouldst till;
And only didst for others plant the vine
Of liberty, not drunken with its wine.   [54 *ll.*

So while our star that gives us light and heat,
Seem'd now a long and gloomy night to threat,
Up from the other world his flame doth dart,
And princes, shining through their windows, start;
Who their suspected counsellors refuse,
And credulous ambassadors accuse:
" Is this," saith one, " the nation that we read,
" Spent with both wars, under a captain dead!
" Yet rig a navy, while we dress us late,
" And ere we dine, rase and rebuild a state?
" What oaken forests, and what golden mines!
" What mints of men, what union of designs!   [10 *ll.*
" What refuge to escape them can be found,
" Whose watery leaguers all the world surround?
" Needs must we all their tributaries be,
" Whose navies hold the sluices of the sea!
" The ocean is the fountain of command,
" But that once took, we captives are on land;
" And those that have the waters for their share,
" Can quickly leave us neither earth nor air;
" Yet if through these our fears could find a pass
" Through double oak, and lined with treble brass;
" That one man still, although but named, alarms
" More than all men, all navies, and all arms;
" Him all the day, him in late nights I dread,
" And still his sword seems hanging o'er my head.

" The nation had been ours, but his one soul
" Moves the great bulk, and animates the whole,
" He secrecy with number hath inchased,
" Courage with age, maturity with haste ;
" The valiant's terror, riddle of the wise,
" And still his falchion all our knots unties.
" Where did he learn those arts that cost us dear ?
" Where below earth, or where above the sphere ?
" He seems a king by long succession born,
" And yet the same to be a king doth scorn.
" Abroad a king he seems, and something more,
" At home a subject on the equal floor ;
" Or could I once him with our title see,
" So should I hope yet he might die as we.
" But let them write his praise that love him best,
" It grieves me sore to have thus much confest."

Pardon, great Prince, if thus their fear or spite,
More than our love and duty do thee right ;
I yield, nor further will the prize contend,
So that we both alike may miss our end ;
While thou thy venerable head dost raise
As far above their malice as my praise ;
And, as the angel of our commonweal,
Troubling the waters, yearly mak'st them heal.

Andrew Marvell.

UNCAGED.

From " The Mistresse of Philarete."

OR I will for no man's pleasure
Change a syllable or measure :   [4 *ll.*
Pedants shall not tie my strains
To their antique poets' veins.   [2 *ll.*
Being born as free as these,
I will sing as I shall please.   *George Wither.*

TO CYRIAC SKINNER.

(1655.)

YRIAC, this three-years-day these eyes, though
　　clear,
　　To outward view, of blemish or of spot,
Bereft of light, their seeing have forgot,
　Nor to their idle orbs doth sight appear
Of sun, or moon, or star, throughout the year,
　Or man, or woman.　Yet I argue not
　Against Heaven's hand or will, nor hate a jot
　Of heart or hope; but still bear up and steer
Right onward.　What supports me, dost thou ask?
　The conscience, Friend, to have lost them overplied
　In Liberty's defence, my noble task,
Of which all Europe rings from side to side.
　This thought might lead me through the world's vain
　　mask,
　Content though blind, had I no better guide.

John Milton.

ON THE LATE MASSACRE IN PIEMONT.

(1655.)

VENGE, O Lord, thy slaughter'd saints, whose
　　bones
　　Lie scatter'd on the Alpine mountains cold;
　Even them who kept thy truth so pure of old,
　When all our fathers worshipp'd stocks and stones,

Forget not; in thy book record their groans
  Who were thy sheep, and in their ancient fold
  Slain by the bloody Piemontese, that roll'd
Mother with infant down the rocks.   Their moans
The vales redoubled to the hills, and they
  To heaven.   Their martyr'd blood and ashes sow
  O'er all the Italian fields, where still doth sway
The triple tyrant; that from these may grow
  A hundredfold, who, having learn'd thy way,
  Early may fly the Babylonian woe.

John Milton.

ON THE VICTORY OBTAINED BY BLAKE,

*Over the Spaniards, in the Bay of Santa Cruz, in the
Island of Teneriffe,* 1657.

NOW does Spain's fleet her spacious wings unfold,
  Leaves the new world, and hastens for the old;
  But though the wind was fair, they slowly swum,
Freighted with acted guilt, and guilt to come:
For this rich load, of which so proud they are,
Was raised by tyranny, and raised for war.
Every capacious galleon's womb was fill'd
With what the womb of wealthy kingdoms yield;
The new world's wounded entrails they had tore,
For wealth wherewith to wound the old once more,
Wealth which all other's avarice might cloy,
But yet in them caused as much fear as joy.
For now upon the main themselves they saw
That boundless empire, where you give the law;
Of wind's and water's rage they fearful be,
But much more fearful are your flags to see.

Day, that to those who sail upon the deep
More wish'd for and more welcome is than sleep,
They dreaded to behold, lest the sun's light
With English streamers should salute their sight:
In thickest darkness they would choose to steer,
So that such darkness might suppress their fear.
At length it vanishes, and fortune smiles,
For they behold the sweet Canary isles,
One of which doubtless is by nature bless'd
Above both worlds, since 'tis above the rest.
For lest some gloominess might stain her sky,
Trees there the duty of the clouds supply :
O noble trust which heaven on this isle pours,
Fertile to be, yet never need her showers !
A happy people, which at once do gain
The benefits, without the ills, of rain !
Both health and profit fate cannot deny,
Where still the earth is moist, the air still dry.
The jarring elements no discord know,
Fuel and rain together kindly grow ;
And coolness there with heat does never fight,
This only rules by day, and that by night.
Your worth to all these isles a just right brings,
The best of lands should have the best of kings ;
And these want nothing heaven can afford,
Unless it be, the having you their lord.
But this great want will not a long one prove,
Your conquering sword will soon that want remove ;
For Spain had better, she'll ere long confess,
Have broken all her swords, than this one peace.
Casting that league off, which she held so long,
She cast off that which only made her strong,
Forces and art, she soon will feel, are vain,
Peace, against you, was the sole strength of Spain ;

By that alone those islands she secures,
Peace makes them hers, but war will make them yours.
There the rich grape the soil indulgent breeds,
Which of the gods the fancied drink exceeds;
They still do yield, such is their precious mould,
All that is good, and are not cursed with gold;
With fatal gold, for still where that does grow
Neither the soil, nor people, quiet know;
Which troubles men to raise it when 'tis ore,
And when 'tis raised does trouble them much more.
Ah, why was thither brought that cause of war,
Kind nature had from thence removed so far!
In vain doth she those islands free from ill,
If fortune can make guilty what she will.
But whilst I draw that scene, where you, ere long,
Shall conquests act, you present are unsung.

For Santa Cruz the glad fleet takes her way,
And safely there casts anchor in the bay;
Never so many, with one joyful cry,
That place saluted, where they all must die.
Deluded men! Fate with you did but sport,
You 'scaped the sea, to perish in your port;
'Twas more for England's fame you should die there,
Where you had most of strength and least of fear.
The Peak's proud height the Spaniards all admire,
Yet in their breasts carry a pride much higher.
Only to this vast hill a power is given,
At once both to inhabit earth and heaven;
But this stupendous prospect did not near
Make them admire, so much as they did fear.

For here they met with news, which did produce
A grief, above the cure of grape's best juice.

They learn'd with terror, that nor summer's heat,
Nor winter's storms, had made your fleet retreat.
To fight against such foes was vain, they knew,
Which did the rage of elements subdue,
Who on the ocean, that does horror give
To all beside, triumphantly do live.

With haste they therefore all their galleons moor,
And flank with cannon from the neighbouring shore;
Forts, lines, and sconces, all the bay along,
They build, and act all that can make them strong.

Fond men! who know not whilst such works they
     raise,
They only labour to exalt your praise.
Yet they by restless toil became at length
So proud and confident of their made strength,
That they with joy their boasting general heard
Wish then for that assault he lately fear'd.
His wish he had, for now undaunted Blake,
With winged speed, for Santa Cruz does make.
For your renown, the conquering fleet does ride
O'er seas as vast as is the Spaniard's pride;
Whose fleet and trenches view'd, you soon did say,
We to their strength are more obliged than they;
Wer't not for that, they from their fate would run,
And a third world seek out, our arms to shun.
Those forts, which there so high and strong appear,
Do not so much suppress, as show their fear;
Of speedy victory let no man doubt,
Our worst work pass'd, now we have found them out:
Behold their navy does at anchor lie,
And they are ours, for now they cannot fly.

This said, the whole fleet gave it their applause,

And all assume your courage, in your cause.
That bay they enter, which unto them owes
The noblest wreaths which victory bestows;
Bold Stanier leads; this fleet's design'd by fate
To give him laurel, as the last did plate.

The thundering cannon now begins the fight,
And, though it be at noon, creates a night;
The air was soon, after the fight begun,
Far more enflamed by it, than by the sun.
Never so burning was that climate known;
War turn'd the temperate to the torrid zone.

Fate these two fleets, between both worlds, had
    brought,
Who fight, as if for both those worlds they sought.
Thousands of ways, thousands of men there die,
Some ships are sunk, some blown up in the sky.
Nature ne'er made cedars so high aspire
As oaks did then, urged by the active fire
Which, by quick powder's force, so high was sent
That it return'd to its own element.
Torn limbs some leagues into the island fly,
Whilst others lower, in the sea, do lie;
Scarce souls from bodies sever'd are so far
By death, as bodies there were by the war.
The all-seeing sun ne'er gazed on such a sight.
Two dreadful navies there at anchor fight,
And neither have, or power, or will, to fly;
There one must conquer, or there both must die.
Far different motives yet engaged them thus,
Necessity did them, but choice did us,
A choice which did the highest worth express,
And was attended by as high success.

For your resistless genius there did reign,
By which we laurels reap'd e'en on the main :
So prosperous stars, though absent to the sense,
Bless those they shine for by their influence.

Our cannon now tears every ship and sconce,
And o'er two elements triumphs at once ;
Their galleons sunk, their wealth the sea does fill,
The only place where it can cause no ill.

Ah ! would those treasures which both Indias have
Were buried in as large, and deep a grave !
War's chief support with them would buried be,
And the land owe her peace unto the sea.
Ages to come your conquering arms will bless,
There they destroy'd what had destroy'd their peace ;
And in one war the present age may boast,
The certain seeds of many wars are lost.

All the foe's ships destroy'd by sea or fire,
Victorious Blake does from the bay retire.
His siege of Spain he then again pursues,
And there first brings of his success the news ;
The saddest news that e'er to Spain was brought,
Their rich fleet sunk, and ours with laurel fraught,
Whilst fame in every place her trumpet blows,
And tells the world how much to you it owes.

Andrew Marvell.

A POEM UPON THE DEATH OF HIS LATE
HIGHNESS THE LORD PROTECTOR.

THAT Providence which had so long the care
Of Cromwell's head, and number'd every hair,
Now in itself (the glass where all appears)
Had seen the period of his golden years,
And thenceforth only did attend to trace
What death might least so fair a life deface.

The people, which what most they fear esteem,
Death when more horrid so more noble deem,
And blame the last act, like spectators vain,
Unless the Prince whom they applaud be slain.
Nor fate indeed can well refuse the right
To those that lived in war, to die in fight.

But long his valour none had left that could
Endanger him, or clemency that would;
And he (whom nature all for peace had made,
But angry heaven unto war had sway'd,
And so less useful where he most desired,
For what he least affected, was admired)
Deserved yet an end whose every part
Should speak the wondrous softness of his heart.
To Love and Grief the fatal writ was signed,
(Those nobler weaknesses of human kind,
From which those Powers that issued the decree,
Although immortal, found they were not free)
That they to whom his breast still open lies
In gentle passions, should his death disguise,
And leave succeeding ages cause to mourn,
As long as grief shall weep, or love shall burn.

Straight does a slow and languishing disease.
Eliza, Nature's and his darling, seize ;
Her, when an infant, taken with her charms,
He oft would flourish in his mighty arms,
And lest their force the tender burthen wrong,
Slacken the vigour of his muscles strong,
Then to the mother's breast her softly move,
Which, while she drain'd of milk, she fill'd with love.
But as with riper years her virtue grew,
And every minute adds a lustre new ;
When with meridian height her beauty shined
And thorough that sparkled her fairer mind ;
When she with smiles serene, in words discreet,
His hidden soul at every turn could meet :
Then might you've daily his affection spied,
Doubling that knot which destiny had tied,
While they by sense, not knowing, comprehend
How on each other both their fates depend.
With her each day the pleasing hours he shares,
And at her aspect calms his growing cares ;
Or with a grandsire's joy her children sees,
Hanging about her neck, or at his knees.
Hold fast, dear infants, hold them both, or none ;
This will not stay, when once the other's gone.
A silent fire now wastes those limbs of wax,
And him within his tortured image racks ;
So the flower withering which the garden crown'd,
The sad root pines in secret under ground.
Each groan he doubled, and each sigh she sigh'd
Repeated over to the restless night ;
No trembling string, composed to numbers new,
Answers the touch in notes more sad, more true.
She, lest he grieve, hides, what she can, her pains,
And he, to lessen her's, his sorrow feigns ;

Yet both perceived, yet both conceal'd their skills,
And so, diminishing, increased their ills,
That whether by each other's grief they fell,
Or on their own redoubled, none can tell.　　　[34 *ll.*

　　A secret cause does sure those signs ordain,
Foreboding princes' falls, and seldom vain :
Whether some kinder powers, that wish us well,
What they above cannot prevent, foretell ;
Or the great world do by consent presage,
As hollow seas with future tempests rage ;
Or rather Heaven, which us so long foresees,
Their funerals celebrate, while it decrees.
But never yet was any human fate
By nature solemnized with so much state :
He unconcern'd the dreadful passage crost,
But oh ! what pangs that death did Nature cost !

　　First the great thunder was shot off, and sent
The signal from the starry battlement.
The winds receive it, and its force outdo,
As practising how they could thunder too.
Out of the binder's hand the sheaves they tore,
And thrash'd the harvest in the airy floor ;
Or of huge trees, whose growth with his did rise,
The deep foundations open'd to the skies ;
Then heavy showers the winged tempests lead,
And pour the deluge o'er the chaos' head.
The race of warlike horses at his tomb,
Offer themselves in many a hecatomb ;
With pensive head towards the ground they fall,
And helpless languish at the tainted stall.
Numbers of men decrease with pains unknown,
And hasten (not to see his death) their own.

Such tortures all the elements unfix'd,
Troubled to part where so exactly mix'd ;
And as through air his wasting spirits flow'd,
The world with throes labour'd beneath their load.

Nature, it seem'd, with him would nature vie,
He with Eliza, it with him would die.

He without noise still travell'd to his end,
As silent suns to meet the night descend.
The stars, that for him fought, had only power
Left to determine now his fatal hour,
Which since they might not hinder, yet they cast
To choose it worthy of his glories past.
No part of time but bare his mark away
Of honour,—all the year was Cromwell's day ;
But this, of all the most auspicious found,
Twice had in open field him victor crown'd,
When up the armed mountains of Dunbar
He march'd, and through deep Severn, ending war.
What day should him eternize, but the same
That had before immortalized his name,
That so whoe'er would at his death have joy'd,
In their own griefs might find themselves employ'd,
But those that sadly his departure grieved,
Yet joy'd, remembering what he once achieved ?
And the last minute his victorious ghost
Gave chase to Ligny on the Belgic coast :
Ere, ended all his mortal toils, he laid
And slept in peace under the laurel-shade.
   O Cromwell ! Heaven's favourite, to none
Have such high honours from above been shown,
For whom the elements we mourners see,
And Heaven itself would the great herald be,

Which with more care set forth his obsequies
Than those of Moses, hid from human eyes;
As jealous only here, lest all be less
Than we could to his memory express.

Then let us too our course of mourning keep;
Where Heaven leads, 'tis piety to weep.
Stand back ye seas, and shrunk beneath the veil
Of your abyss, with cover'd head bewail
Your monarch. We demand not your supplies
To compass-in our isle,—our tears suffice,
Since him away the dismal tempest rent,
Who once more join'd us to the continent;
Who planted England on the Flanderic shore,
And stretch'd our frontier to the Indian ore;
Whose greater truths obscure the fables old,
Whether of British saints or worthies told,
And in a valour lessening Arthur's deeds,
For holiness the Confessor exceeds.

He first put arms into Religion's hand,
And timorous conscience unto courage mann'd;
The soldier taught that inward mail to wear,
And fearing God, how they should nothing fear.
Those strokes, he said, will pierce through all below,
Where those that strike from Heaven fetch their blow.
Astonish'd armies did their flight prepare,
And cities strong were storméd by his prayer.
Of that for ever Preston's field shall tell
The story, and impregnable Clonmel,
And where the sandy mountain Fenwick scaled,
The sea between, yet hence his prayer prevailed.
What man was ever so in heaven obey'd
Since the commanded sun o'er Gibeon stay'd?

In all his wars, needs must he triumph, when
He conquer'd God still ere he fought with men :
Hence, though in battle none so brave or fierce,
Yet him the adverse steel could never pierce ;
Pity it seem'd to hurt him more, that felt
Each wound himself which he to others dealt,
Danger itself refusing to offend
So loose an enemy, so fast a friend.
Friendship, that sacred virtue, long does claim
The first foundation of his house and name :
But within one its narrow limits fall,
His tenderness extended unto all,
And that deep soul through every channel flows,
Where kindly Nature loves itself to lose.
More strong affections never reason served,
Yet still affected most what best deserved.
If he Eliza loved to that degree,
(Though who more worthy to be loved than she ?)
If so indulgent to his own, how dear
To him the children of the Highest were !
For her he once did Nature's tribute pay ;
For these his life adventured every day :
And 'twould be found, could we his thoughts have cast,
Their griefs struck deepest, if Eliza's last.
What prudence more than human did he need
To keep so dear, so differing minds agreed ?
The worser sort, so conscious of their ill,
Lie weak and easy to the ruler's will :
But to the good (too many or too few)
All law is useless, all reward is due.
Ah ! ill-advised, if not for love, for shame,
Spare yet your own, if you neglect his fame ;
Lest others dare to think your zeal a mask,
And you to govern only Heaven's task.

Valour, Religion, Friendship, Prudence died
At once with him, and all that's good beside;
And we, Death's refuge, Nature's dregs, confined
To loathsome life, alas! are left behind.
Where we (so once we used) shall now no more,
To fetch day, press about his chamber-door,
From which he issued with that awful state,
It seem'd Mars broke through Janus' double gate,
Yet always temper'd with an air so mild,
No April suns that e'er so gently smiled;
No more shall hear that powerful language charm,
Whose force oft spared the labour of his arm;
No more shall follow where he spent the days
In war, in counsel, or in prayer and praise,
Whose meanest acts he would himself advance,
As ungirt David to the ark did dance.
All, all is gone of ours or his delight
In horses fierce, wild deer, or armour bright;
Francisca fair can nothing now but weep,
Nor with soft notes shall sing his cares asleep.

  I saw him dead: a leaden slumber lies,
And mortal sleep over those wakeful eyes;
Those gentle rays under the lids were fled,
Which through his looks that piercing sweetness
        shed;
That port, which so majestic was and strong,
Loose, and deprived of vigour, stretch'd along;
All wither'd, all discolour'd, pale and wan,
How much another thing; no more that Man!
O, human glory vain, O, Death, O, wings!
O, worthless world, O, transitory things!
Yet dwelt that greatness in his shape decay'd,
That still, though dead, greater than death he laid;

And in his alter'd face you something feign
That threatens death he yet will live again.
Not much unlike the sacred oak, which shoots
To heaven its branches, and through earth its roots,
Whose spacious boughs are hung with trophies round,
And honour'd wreaths have oft the victor crown'd ;
When angry Jove darts lightning through the air
At mortal sins, nor his own plant will spare,
It groans and bruises all below, that stood
So many years the shelter of the wood,
The tree, erewhile foreshorten'd to our view,
When fall'n shows taller yet than as it grew.
So shall his praise to after times increase,
When truth shall be allow'd, and faction cease.
And his own shadows with him fall ; the eye
Detracts from objects than itself more high ;
But when Death takes them from that envied state,—
Seeing how little, we confess how great.

Thee, many ages hence, in martial verse
Shall the English soldier, ere he charge, rehearse ;
Singing of thee, inflame himself to fight,
And, with the name of Cromwell, armies fright.
As long as rivers to the seas shall run,
As long as Cynthia shall relieve the sun,
While stags shall fly unto the forests thick,
While sheep delight the grassy downs to pick,
As long as future time succeeds the past,
Always thy honour, praise, and name shall last !   [38 *ll.*

Andrew Marvell.

ROYAL RESOLUTIONS.

I.

WHEN plate was at pawn, and fob at an ebb,
    And spider might weave in bowels its web,
    And stomach as empty as brain;
Then Charles without acre,
Did swear by his Maker,
If e'er I see England again,
I'll have a religion all of my own,
Whether Popish or Protestant shall not be known;
And if it prove troublesome, I will have none.

II.

I'll have a long parliament always to friend,
And furnish my treasure as fast as I spend,
And if they will not, they shall have an end.   [1 st.

IV.

My insolent brother shall bear all the sway;
If parliaments murmur, I'll send him away;
And call him again as soon as I may.   [2 st.

VII.

The ancient nobility I will lay by,
And new ones create their rooms to supply,
And they shall raise fortunes for my own fry.

VIII.

Some one I'll advance from a common descent,
So high that he shall hector the parliament,
And all wholesome laws for the public prevent,

o

IX.

And I will assert him to such a degree
That all his foul treasons, though daring and high,
Under my hand and seal shall have indemnity.   [3 *st.*

XIII.

I'll wholly abandon all public affairs,
And pass all my time with buffoons and players,
And saunter to Nelly when I should be at prayers.

XIV.

I'll have a fine pond with a pretty decoy,
Where many strange fowl shall feed and enjoy,
And still in their language quack *Vive le Roy!*

Andrew Marvell.

THE CONTENTED MAN'S MORRICE.

(*From Speculum Speculativum*, 1660.)

THESE words in youth my motto were,   [3 *st.*
    And mine in age I'll make them,
        I neither Have, nor Want, nor Care ;
When also first I spake them,
    I thought things would be as they are,
And meekly, therefore, take them.

The riches I possess this day
    Are no such goods of fortune
As king can give or take away,
    Or tyrants make uncertain ;
For hid within myself they are,
    Behind an unseen curtain.

Of my degree but few or none
    Were daily so frequented;
But now I'm left of every one,
    And therewith well contented.
For when I am with God alone,
    Much folly is prevented.

Then why should I give way to grief?
    Come, strike up pipe and tabor;
He that affecteth God in chief,
    And as himself his neighbour,
May still enjoy a happy life,
    Although he lives by labour.   [5 *st.*

For service done and love exprest,
    Though very few regard it,
My country owes me bread at least;
    But, if I be debarr'd it,
Good conscience is a daily feast,
    And sorrow never marr'd it.   [4 *st.*

There is no trust in temp'ral things,
    For they are all unsteady:
That no assurance from them springs,
    Too well I find already;
And that e'en parliaments and kings,
    Are frail, or false, or giddy.

All stands upon a tott'ring wheel,
    Which never fix'd abideth;
Both Commonweals and Kingdoms reel:
    He that in them confideth
(Or trust their faith) shall mischief feel,
    With which soe'er he sideth.   [6 *st.*

This only doth my mirth allay,
   I am to some engaged
Who sigh and weep, and suffer may
   Whilst thus I sing encaged :
But I've a God, and so have they,
   By whom that care's assuaged.

And he that gives us in these days
   New Lords may give us new laws ;
So that our present puppet-plays,
   Our whimsies, brawls, and gewgaws,
May turned be to songs of praise,
   And holy hallelujahs.

George Wither.

FROM SAMSON AGONISTES.

The Day of Deliverance.

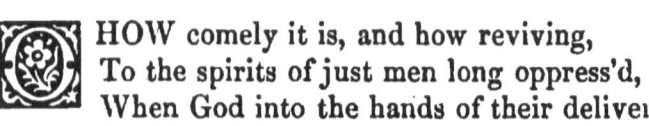 HOW comely it is, and how reviving,
   To the spirits of just men long oppress'd,
   When God into the hands of their deliverer
Puts invincible might,
To quell the mighty of the earth, the oppressor,
The brute and boisterous force of violent men,
Hardy and industrious to support
Tyrannic power, but raging to pursue
The righteous, and all such as honour truth.

The Day of Doubt.

GOD of our fathers, what is man!
   That thou toward him with hand so various—
   Or might I say contrarious,
Temper'st thy providence through his short course;
Not evenly, as thou rulest
The angelic orders and inferior creatures mute,
Irrational and brute.
Nor do I name of men the common rout,
That, wandering loose about,
Grow up and perish, as the summer-fly,
Heads without name, no more remember'd;
But such as thou hast solemnly elected,
With gifts and graces eminently adorn'd,
To some great work, thy glory,
And people's safety, which in part they effect:
Yet toward these thus dignified, thou oft,
Amidst their height of noon,
Changest thy countenance, and thy hand, with no regard
Of highest favours past
From thee on them, or them to thee of service.
   Nor only dost degrade them, or remit
To life obscured, which were a fair dismission;
But throw'st them lower than thou didst exalt them
      high,
Unseemly falls in human eye,
Too grievous for the trespass or omission;
Oft leavest them to the hostile sword
Of heathen and profane, their carcasses
To dogs and fowls a prey, or else captiv'd;
Or to the unjust tribunals, under change of times,
And condemnation of the ingrateful multitude.

If these they 'scape, perhaps in poverty
With sickness and disease thou bow'st them down,
Painful diseases and deformed,
In crude old age ;
Though not disordinate, yet causeless suffering
The punishment of dissolute days.   In fine,
Just or unjust, alike seem miserable,
For oft alike both come to evil end.

The Close.

LL is best, though we oft doubt
What the unsearchable dispose
Of Highest Wisdom brings about,
And ever best found in the close.
Oft He seems to hide His face,
But unexpectedly returns,
And to his faithful champion hath in place
Bore witness gloriously ; whence Gaza mourns,
And all that band them to resist
His uncontrollable intent ;
His servants He, with new acquist
Of true experience from this great event,
With peace and consolation hath dismiss'd,
And calm of mind, all passion spent.

John Milton.

NOTES.

PAGE 23. *On his Majesty's receiving the news of the Duke of Buckingham's assassination.* He "was at the public prayers of the Church, when Sir John Hippesley came into the room, with a troubled countenance, and without any pause, in respect of the exercise they were performing, went directly to the king and whispered in his ear what had fallen out. His Majesty continued unmoved, and without the least change in his countenance, till prayers were ended."—*Clarendon.*

Page 87. *The Arrest of the Five Members.* "Force was to be met by force; and when Charles and his armed attendants passed through the lobby of the House of Commons, on the 4th of January, the Civil War had substantially begun. Clarendon himself admits as much when he calls it 'the most visible introduction to all the misery that afterwards befel the king and kingdom.'"—*Forster's "Arrest of the Five Members."*

Page 89. *Keinton* is another name for Edgehill, the first great battle of the Civil War.

Page 95. *A Western Wonder.* Before the battle of Edgehill the Parliament, entirely possessed of Devonshire, drew its forces to Launceston to catch Sir Ralph Hopton and his adherents. Hopton raised 3000 men "for the dispersing of that unlawful assembly at Launceston." Sir George Chadleigh, a gentleman of fortune in the county, upon the news of Hopton's advance came with five or six troops of horse within three miles of Launceston. But the Parliament force quitted Launceston that night. Hopton entered next morning, and he and his men presently became masters of Cornwall. Hopton and his Cornishmen having presently afterwards defeated a Parliamentary force at Bradoch Down, the Earl of Stamford retired into Tavistock to protect a part of Devonshire, but on Hopton's approach quitted Tavistock in haste, some of his force going to Plymouth, some to Exeter.

Page 107. *When the king enjoys his own again.* Booker, Pond, Hammond, Rivers, Swallow, Dade, and the Man in the Moon, were names attached to the astrological almanacs of the day.

Page 162. *On the New Forces of Conscience.* "A. S." answered, in 1643, a pamphlet in which the Independents argued on behalf of toleration. Samuel Rutherford was a Scotch Divinity professor who took part in the settlement of points of Presbyterian discipline, and afterwards showed his temper in a "Disputation on Pretended Liberty of Conscience."

Page 173. *Hurried thy horses.* The wits and poets of the time made much of the incident of Cromwell's being thrown from his coach in the park (Sept. 1654) while driving a runaway team of six Friesland horses which had been given to him by the Duke of Oldenburg.

An Epitaph.

He whom Heaven did call away
Out of this Hermitage of clay,
Has left some reliques in this Urne
As a pledge of his returne.
Meane while yᵉ Muses doe deplore
The losse of this their paramour
Wᵗʰ whom he sported ere yᵉ day
Budded forth its tender ray.
And now Apollo leaues his laies
And puts on cypres for his bayes.
The sacred sisters tune their quills
Onely to yᵉ blubbering rills
And whilst his doome they thinke upon
Make their owne teares their Helicon.
Leaving yᵉ two-topt mount divine
To turne votaries to his shrine.
Thinke not (reader) mee lesse blest
Sleeping in this narrow cist
Than if my ashes did lie hid
Under some stately pyramid.
If a rich tombe makes happy, yᵉ
That Bee was happier far yᵉ men
Who busie in yᵉ thymie wood
Was fettered by yᵉ golden flood,
Wch frō yᵉ Amber-weeping Tree
Distilleth downe so plenteously.
ffor so this little wanton Elfe
Most gloriously enshrind itselfe.
A tombe whose beauty might compare
Wᵗʰ Cleopatra`s sepulcher.
    In this little bed my dust
Incurtaind round I here entrust,
Whilst my more pure and nobler part
Lyes entomb`d in every heart.
    Then pass on gently ye yᵉ mourne,
Touch not this mine hollow`d Urne

When this cold numnes
shall retreate
By a more yⁿ chymick
heat.
[J.] M. 10ᵇᵉʳ. 1647.

This plant, th[us] calcind into dust
In its Ashes rest it must.
Untill sweet Psyche shall Inspire
A softning and [pro]lifick fire
And in her fostring arms enfold
This Heavy and this earthy mould
Then, as I am Ile be no more
But bloome and blossome .. b .s....

These Ashes wᶜʰ doe here remaine
A vitall tincture still retaine
A seminall forme within yᵉ deeps
Of this little chaos sleeps.
The thred of life untwisted is
Into its first consistencies;
Infant nāure cradled here
In its principles appeare.

A List of Books

PUBLISHING BY

SAMPSON LOW, SON, AND MARSTON,

Crown Buildings, 188, Fleet Street.

[*May*, 1868.

NEW ILLUSTRATED WORKS.

THE STORY WITHOUT AN END. From the German of Carové. By Sarah Austin. Illustrated with Sixteen Original Water-Colour Drawings by E. V. B., printed in Fac-simile and numerous Illustrations on wood. Small 4to. cloth extra, 12s.; or inlaid on side with floral ornament on ivory, 15s.; or in morocco, 21s.

*** Also a Large Paper Edition, with the Plates mounted (only 250 copies printed), morocco, ivory inlaid, 31s. 6d.

"*Nowhere will he find the Book of Nature more freshly and beautifully opened for him than in 'The Story without an End,' of its kind one of the best that was ever written.*"—Quarterly Review.

"*We have here a most beautiful edition of Mrs. Austin's well-known translation of 'The Story without an End,' illustrated by E. V. B. with even more than her accustomed poetical grace and fancy. It is difficult to select when all the illustrations are so delicately beautiful, but we cannot help pointing out several that strike us especially. . . . But it is quite impossible to describe these illustrations. We must refer our readers to the book itself if they wish to see a perfect development of the grace, fancy, and true poetical genius for which the pictures of E. V. B. have long been remarkable.*"—Spectator.

"*The illustrations are worthy of the text, for they are generally coloured in strict accordance with nature, and have been printed with marvellous skill. Indeed, we do not hesitate to say that the plates in this volume are the best specimens of colour-printing we have ever seen.*"—Illustrated Times.

Also, illustrated by the same Artist,

Child's Play. Printed in fac-simile from Water-Colour Drawings, 7s. 6d. Tennyson's May Queen. Illustrated on Wood. Large Paper Edition, 7s. 6d.

CHRISTIAN LYRICS. Chiefly selected from Modern Authors.

138 Poems, illustrated with upwards of 150 Engravings, under the superintendence of J. D. Cooper. Small 4to. cloth extra, 10s. 6d.; morocco, 21s.

The Poetry of Nature. Selected and Illustrated with Thirty-six Engravings by Harrison Weir. Crown 8vo. handsomely bound in cloth, gilt edges, 5s.; morocco, 10s. 6d.

*** Forming the new volume of Low's Choice Editions of Choice Books.

Choice Editions of Choice Books. New Editions. Illustrated by C. W. Cope, R. A., T. Creswick, R. A., Edward Duncan, Birket Foster, J. C. Horsley, A. R. A., George Hicks, R. Redgrave, R.A., C. Stonehouse, F. Tayler, George Thomas, H. J. Townshend, E. H. Wehnert, Harrison Weir, &c. Crown 8vo. cloth, 5s. each; mor. 10s. 6d.

Bloomfield's Farmer's Boy.	Keat's Eve of St. Agnes.
Campbell's Pleasures of Hope.	Milton's l'Allegro.
Cundall's Elizabethan Poetry.	Poetry of Nature.
Coleridge's Ancient Mariner.	Roger's Pleasures of Memory.
Goldsmith's Deserted Village.	Shakespeare's Songs and Sonnets.
Goldsmith's Vicar of Wakefield.	Tennyson's May Queen.
Gray's Elegy in a Churchyard.	Wordsworth's Pastoral Poems.

"*Such works are a glorious beatification for a poet. Such 'works as these educate townsmen, who, surrounded by dead and artificial things, as country people are by life and nature, scarcely learn to look at nature till taught by these concentrated specimens of her beauty.*"—Athenæum.

Bishop Heber's Hymns. An Illustrated Edition, with upwards of one hundred Designs. Engraved, in the first style of Art under the superintendence of J. D. Cooper. Small 4to. handsomely bound, price Half a Guinea; morocco, 21s.

The Divine and Moral Songs of Dr. Watts: a New and very choice Edition. Illustrated with One Hundred Woodcuts in the first style of the Art, from Original Designs by Eminent Artists; engraved by J. D. Cooper. Small 4to. cloth extra, price 7s. 6d.; morocco, 15s.

Artists and Arabs; or Sketching in Sunshine. By Henry Blackburn, author of "The Pyrenees," &c. Numerous Illustrations. Demy 8vo. cloth. 10s. 6d.

The Pyrenees; a Description of Summer Life at French Watering Places. By Henry Blackburn, author of "Travelling in Spain in the Present Day." With upwards of 100 Illustrations by Gustave Doré. Royal 8vo, cloth, 18s.; morocco, 25s.

Travelling in Spain in the present day by a party of Ladies and Gentlemen. By the same Author. With numerous Illustrations and Map of Route. Square 8vo. 16s.

Two Centuries of Song; or, Melodies, Madrigals, Sonnets, and other Occasional Verse of the English Poets of the last 200 years. With Critical and Biographical Notes by Walter Thornbury. Illustrated by Original Pictures of Eminent Artists, Drawn and Engraved especially for this work. Printed on toned paper, with coloured borders, designed by Henry Shaw, F.S.A. Very handsomely bound. Cloth extra, 21s.; morocco, 42s.

Milton's Paradise Lost. With the original Steel Engravings of John Martin. Printed on large paper, royal 4to. handsomely bound, 3*l.* 13*s.* 6*d.*; morocco extra, 5*l.* 15*s.* 6*d.*

Light after Darkness: Religious Poems by Harriet Beecher Stowe. With Illustrations. Small post 8vo. cloth, 3*s.* 6*d.*

Poems of the Inner Life. Selected chiefly from modern Authors, by permission. Small post 8vo. 6*s.*; gilt edges, 6*s.* 6*d.*

Favourite English Poems. *Complete Edition.* Comprising a Collection of the most celebrated Poems in the English Language, with but one or two exceptions unabridged, from Chaucer to Tennyson. With 300 Illustrations by the first Artists. Two vols. royal 8vo. half bound, top gilt, Roxburgh style, 1*l.* 18*s.*; antique calf, 3*l.* 3*s.*

. Either Volume sold separately as distinct works. 1. " Early English Poems, Chaucer to Dyer." 2. " Favourite English Poems, Thomson to Tennyson." Each handsomely bound in cloth, 1*l.* 1*s.*

" One of the choicest gift-books of the year, " Favourite English Poems" is not a toy book, to be laid for a week on the Christmas table and then thrown aside with the sparkling trifles of the Christmas tree, but an honest book, to be admired in the season of pleasant remembrances for its artistic beauty; and, when the holydays are over, to be placed for frequent and affectionate consultation on a favourite shelf."—Athenæum.

Schiller's Lay of the Bell. Sir E. Bulwer Lytton's translation; beautifully illustrated by forty-two wood Engravings, drawn by Thomas Scott, and engraved by J. D. Cooper, after the Etchings by Retszch. Oblong 4to. cloth extra, 14*s.*; morocco, 25*s.*

An Entirely New Edition of Edgar A. Poe's Poems. Illustrated by Eminent Artists. Small 4to. cloth extra, price 10*s.* 6*d.*

A History of Lace, from the Earliest Period; with upwards of One Hundred Illustrations and Coloured Designs. By Mrs. Bury Palliser. One volume, 8vo. choicely bound in cloth. 31*s.* 6*d.*

The Royal Cookery Book. By Jules Gouffe, Chef de Cuisine of the Paris Jockey Club. Translated and Adapted for English use. By Alphonse Gouffé, Head Pastrycook to Her Majesty the Queen. Illustrated with large Plates beautifully printed in Colours, and One Hundred and Sixty-One Woodcuts. One volume, super-royal 8vo. cloth extra, 2*l.* 2*s.*

The Bayard Series.

CHOICE COMPANIONABLE BOOKS
FOR HOME AND ABROAD,

COMPRISING

HISTORY, BIOGRAPHY, TRAVEL, ESSAYS,
NOVELETTES, ETC.

Which, under an Editor of known taste and ability, will be ver; choicely printed at the Chiswick Press; with Vignette Title-page Notes, and Index; the aim being to insure permanent value, a well as present attractiveness, and to render each volume an ac quisition to the libraries of a new generation of readers. Size, handsome 16mo. bound flexible in cloth extra, gilt edges averaging about 220 pages.

Each Volume, complete in itself, price Half-a-crown.

THE STORY OF THE CHEVALIER BAYARD. From the French of the Loyal Servant, M. de Berville, and others. By E Walford. With Introduction and Notes by the Editor.

> " Praise of him must walk the earth
> For ever, and to noble deeds give birth.
> This is the happy warrior; this is he
> That every man in arms would wish to be."—*Wordsworth.*

SAINT LOUIS, KING OF FRANCE. The curious an characteristic Life of this Monarch by De Joinville. Translated b James Hutton.

> " *St. Louis and his companions, as described by Joinville, not only i their glistening armour, but in their every-day attire, are brought neare to us, become intelligible to us, and teach us lessons of humanity which u can learn from men only, and not from saints and heroes. Here lies th real value of real history. It widens our minds and our hearts, and give us that true knowledge of the world and of human nature in all its phase which but few can gain in the short span of their own life, and in the nar row sphere of their friends and enemies. We can hardly imagine a bett book for boys to read or for men to ponder over.*"—Times.

The Bayard Series,—

THE ESSAYS OF ABRAHAM COWLEY. Comprising all his Prose Works; the Celebrated Character of Cromwell, Cutter of Coleman Street, &c. &c. With Life, Notes, and Illustrations by Dr. Hurd and others. Newly edited.

" Praised in his day as a great Poet ; the head of the school of poets called metaphysical, he is now chiefly known by those prose essays, all too short, and all too few, which, whether for thought or for expression, have rarely been excelled by any writer in any language."—Mary Russell Mitford's Recollections.

"Cowley's prose stamps him as a man of genius, and an improver of the English language."—Thos. Campbell.

ABDALLAH AND THE FOUR-LEAVED SHAMROCK. By Edouard Laboullaye, of the French Academy. Translated by Mary L. Booth.

One of the noblest and purest French stories ever written.

TABLE-TALK AND OPINIONS OF NAPOLEON THE FIRST.

A compilation from the best sources of this great man's shrewd and often prophetic thoughts, forming the best inner life of the most extraordinary man of modern times.

VATHEK, by William Beckford.

In preparation.

CAVALIER AND PURITAN SONGS, by Henry Morley.

" If the publishers go on as they have begun, they will have furnished us with one of the most valuable and attractive series of books that have ever been issued from the press."—Sunday Times.

" There has, perhaps, never been produced anything more admirable either as regards matter or manner."—Oxford Times.

"' The Bayard Series' is a perfect marvel of cheapness and of exquisite taste in the binding and getting up. We hope and believe that these delicate morsels of choice literature will be widely and gratefully welcomed."

Nonconformist.

The Gentle Life Series.

Printed in Elzevir, on Toned Paper, and handsomely bound,

forming suitable Volumes for Presents.

Price 6s. each; or in calf extra, price 10s. 6d.

I.

THE GENTLE LIFE.   Essays in Aid of the Formation of Character of Gentlemen and Gentlewomen. Seventh Edition.

> " *His notion of a gentleman is of the noblest and truest order. . . . . The volume is a capital specimen of what may be done by honest reason, high feeling, and cultivated intellect. . . . A little compendium of cheerful philosophy.*"—Daily News.
>
> " *Deserves to be printed in letters of gold, and circulated in every house.*"—Chambers's Journal.
>
> " *The writer's object is to teach people to be truthful, sincere, generous : to be humble-minded, but bold in thought and action.*"—Spectator.
>
> " *Full of truth and persuasiveness, the book is a valuable composition, and one to which the reader will often turn for companionship.*"—Morning Post.
>
> " *It is with the more satisfaction that we meet with a new essayist who delights without the smallest pedantry to quote the choicest wisdom of our forefathers, and who abides by those old-fashioned Christian ideas of duty which Steele and Addison, wits and men of the world, were not ashamed to set before the young Englishmen of 1713.*"—London Review.

II.

ABOUT IN THE WORLD.   Essays by the Author of " The Gentle Life."

> " *It is not easy to open it at any page without finding some happy idea.*" Morning Post.
>
> " *Another characteristic merit of these essays is, that they make it their business, gently but firmly, to apply the qualifications and the corrections, which all philanthropic theories, all general rules or maxims, or principles, stand in need of before you can make them work.*"—Literary Churchman.

III.

FAMILIAR WORDS. An Index Verborum, or Quotation Handbook. Affording an immediate Reference to Phrases and Sentences that have become embedded in the English language. Second and enlarged Edition.

" *Should be on every library table, by the side of ' Roget's Thesaurus.' "* —Daily News.

" *Almost every familiar quotation is to be found in this work, which forms a book of reference absolutely indispensable to the literary man, and of interest and service to the public generally. Mr. Friswell has our best thanks for his painstaking, laborious, and conscientious work.*"—City Press.

IV.

LIKE UNTO CHRIST. A new translation of the " De Imitatione Christi," usually ascribed to Thomas à Kempis. With a Vignette from an Original Drawing by Sir Thomas Lawrence.

" *Think of the little work of Thomas à Kempis, translated into a hundred languages, and sold by millions of copies, and which, in inmost moments of deep thought, men make the guide of their hearts, and the friend of their closets.*"—Archbishop of York, at the Literary Fund, 1865.

V.

ESSAYS BY MONTAIGNE. Edited, Compared, Revised, and Annotated by the Author of " The Gentle Life." With Vignette Portrait.

" *The reader really gets in a compact form all of the charming, chatty Montaigne that he needs to know.*"—Observer.

" *We should be glad if any words of ours could help to bespeak a large circulation for this handsome attractive book ; and who can refuse his homage to the good-humoured industry of the editor.*"—Illustrated Times.

VI.

THE COUNTESS OF PEMBROKE'S ARCADIA. Written by Sir Philip Sidney. Edited, with Notes, by the Author of " The Gentle Life." Dedicated, by permission, to the Earl of Derby. 7s. 6d.

" *All the best things in the Arcadia are retained intact in Mr. Friswell's edition, and even brought into greater prominence than in the original, by the curtailment of some of its inferior portions, and the omission of most of its eclogues and other metrical digressions.*"—Examiner.

" *The book is now presented to the modern reader in a shape the most likely to be acceptable in these days of much literature and fastidious taste.*"—Daily News.

" *It was in itself a thing so interesting as a development of English literature, that we are thankful to Mr. Friswell for reproducing, in a very elegant volume, the chief work of the gallant and chivalrous, the gay yet learned knight, who patronized the muse of Spenser, and fell upon the bloody field of Zutphen, leaving behind him a light of heroism and humane compassion which would shed an eternal glory on his name, though all he ever wrote had perished with himself.*"—London Review.

VII.

THE GENTLE LIFE. Second Series.

"*There is the same mingled power and simplicity which makes the author so emphatically a first-rate essayist, giving a fascination in each essay which will make this volume at least as popular as its elder brother.*" Star.

"*These essays are amongst the best in our language.*"—Public Opinion.

VIII.

VARIA: Readings from Rare Books. Reprinted, by permission, from the *Saturday Review, Spectator,* &c.

CONTENTS:—The Angelic Doctor, Nostradamus, Thomas à Kempis, Dr. John Faustus, Quevedo, Mad. Guyon, Paracelsus, Howell the Traveller, Michael Scott, Lodowick Muggleton, Sir Thomas Browne, George Psalmanazar, The Highwaymen, The Spirit World.

"*The books discussed in this volume are no less valuable than they are rare, but life is not long enough to allow a reader to wade through such thick folios, and therefore the compiler is entitled to the gratitude of the public for having sifted their contents, and thereby rendered their treasures available to the general reader.*"—Observer.

IX.

A CONCORDANCE OR VERBAL INDEX to the whole of Milton's Poetical Works. Comprising upwards of 20,000 References. By Charles D. Cleveland, LL.D. With Vignette Portrait of Milton.

₊ This work affords an immediate reference to any passage in any edition of Milton's Poems, to which it may be justly termed an indispensable Appendix.

"*An invaluable Index, which the publishers have done a public service in reprinting.*"—Notes and Queries.

X.

THE SILENT HOUR: Essays, Original and Selected. By the Author of "The Gentle Life."

CONTENTS.

How to read the Scriptures	From the Homilies.
Unreasonable Infidelity	Isaac Barrow.
The Great Loss of the Worldling . . .	Richard Baxter.
Certainty of Death	Dean Sherlock.
On the Greatness of God	Massillon.
Our Daily Bread	Bishop Latimer.
The Art of Contentment	Archbishop Sandys.
The Foolish Exchange	Jeremy Taylor.
Of a Peaceable Temper	Isaac Barrow.
On the Marriage Ring	Jeremy Taylor.
Nearer to God	Archbishop Sandys.
The Sanctity of Home	John Ruskin.
The Thankful Heart	Isaak Walton.
Silence, Meditation, and Rest.	

And other Essays by the Editor. Second Edition. Nearly ready.

LITERATURE, WORKS OF REFERENCE ETC.

HE Origin and History of the English Language, and of the early literature it embodies. By the Hon. George P. Marsh, U. S. Minister at Turin, Author of " Lectures on the English Language." 8vo. cloth extra, 16s.

Lectures on the English Language; forming the Introductory Series to the foregoing Work. By the same Author. 8vo. Cloth, 16s. This is the only author's edition.

Man and Nature; or, Physical Geography as Modified by Human Action. By George P. Marsh, Author of " Lectures on the English Language," &c. 8vo. cloth, 14s.

> " *Mr. Marsh, well known as the author of two of the most scholarly works yet published·on the English language, sets himself in excellent spirit, and with immense learning, to indicate the character, and, approximately, the extent of the changes produced by human action in the physical condition of the globe we inhabit. In four divisions of his work, Mr. Marsh traces the history of human industry as shown in the extensive modification and extirpation of animal and vegetable life in the woods, the waters, and the sands; and, in a concluding chapter, he discusses the probable and possible geographical changes yet to be wrought. The whole of Mr. Marsh's book is an eloquent showing of the duty of care in the establishment of harmony between man's life and the forces of nature, so as to bring to their highest points the fertility of the soil, the vigour of the animal life, and the salubrity of the climate, on which we have to depend for the physical well-being of mankind.*"—Examiner.

Her Majesty's Mails: a History of the Post Office, and an Industrial Account of its Present Condition. By Wm. Lewins, of the General Post Office. 2nd edition, revised, and enlarged, with a Photographic Portrait of Sir Rowland Hill. Small post 8vo. 6s.

> " *Will take its stand as a really useful book of reference on the history of the Post. We heartily recommend it as a thoroughly careful performance.*"—Saturday Review.

A History of Banks for Savings; including a full account of the origin and progress of Mr. Gladstone's recent prudential measures. By William Lewins, Author of " Her Majesty's Mails." 8vo. cloth. 12s.

The English Catalogue of Books: giving the date of publication of every book published from 1835 to 1863, in addition to the title, size, price, and publisher, in one alphabet. An entirely new work, combining the Copyrights of the " London Catalogue" and the " British Catalogue." One thick volume of 900 pages, half morocco, 45s.

Index to the Subjects of Books published in the United Kingdom during the last Twenty Years—1837-1857. · Containing as many as 74,000 references, under subjects, so as to ensure immediate reference to the books on the subject required, each giving title, price, publisher, and date. Two valuable Appendices are also given—A, containing full lists of all Libraries, Collections, Series, and Miscellanies—and B, a List of Literary Societies, Printing Societies, and their Issues. One vol. royal 8vo. Morocco, 1*l.* 6*s.*

A Dictionary of Photography, on the Basis of Sutton's Dictionary. Rewritten by Professor Dawson, of King's College. Editor of the "Journal of Photography;" and Thomas Sutton, B.A., Editor of "Photograph Notes." 8vo. with numerous Illustrations. 8*s.* 6*d.*

Dr. Worcester's New and Greatly Enlarged Dictionary of the English Language. Adapted for Library or College Reference, comprising 40,000 Words more than Johnson's Dictionary, and 250 pages more than the Quarto Edition of Webster's Dictionary. In one Volume, royal 4to. cloth, 1,834 pp. price 31*s.* 6*d.* Half russia, 2*l.* 2*s.* The Cheapest Book ever published.

"The volumes before us show a vast amount of diligence; but with Webster it is diligence in combination with fancifulness,—with Worcester in combination with good sense and judgment. Worcester's is the soberer and safer book, and may be pronounced the best existing English Lexicon."—*Athenæum.*

The Publishers' Circular, and General Record of British and Foreign Literature; giving a transcript of the title-page of every work published in Great Britain, and every work of interest published abroad, with lists of all the publishing houses.

Published regularly on the 1st and 15th of every Month, and forwarded post free to all parts of the world on payment of 8*s.* per annum.

A Handbook to the Charities of London. By Sampson Low, Jun. Comprising an Account of upwards of 800 Institutions chiefly in London and its Vicinity. A Guide to the Benevolent and to the Unfortunate. Cloth limp, 1*s.* 6*d.*

Prince Albert's Golden Precepts. *Second Edition,* with Photograph. A Memorial of the Prince Consort; comprising Maxims and Extracts from Addresses of His late Royal Highness. Many now for the first time collected and carefully arranged. With an Index. Royal 16mo. beautifully printed on toned paper, cloth, gilt edges, 2*s.* 6*d.*

Our Little Ones in Heaven: Thoughts in Prose and Verse, selected from the Writings of favourite Authors; with Frontispiece after Sir Joshua Reynolds. Fcap. 8vo. cloth extra, 3*s.* 6*d.*

Rural Essays. With Practical Hints on Farming and Agricultural Architecture. By Ik. Marvel, Author of "Reveries of a Bachelor." 1 vol. post 8vo. with numerous Illustrations. 8*s.*

The Book of the Hand; or, the Science of Modern Palmistry. Chiefly according to the Systems of D'Arpentigny and Desbarolles. By A. R. Craig, M.A. Crown 8vo. 7*s.* 6*d.*

BIOGRAPHY, TRAVEL, AND ADVENTURE.

THE Life of John James Audubon, the Naturalist, including his Romantic Adventures in the back woods of America, Correspondence with celebrated Europeans, &c. Edited, from materials supplied by his widow, by Robert Buchanan. 8vo.   [*Shortly.*

Christian Heroes in the Army and Navy. By Charles Rogers, LL.D. Author of "Lyra Britannica." Crown 8vo. 3s. 6d.

Leopold the First, King of the Belgians; from unpublished documents, by Theodore Juste. Translated by Robert Black, M.A   [*In preparation.*

Fredrika Bremer's Life, Letters, and Posthumous Works. Edited by her sister, Charlotte Bremer; translated from the Swedish by Fred. Milow. Post 8vo. cloth. 10s. 6d.

The Rise and Fall of the Emperor Maximilian: an Authentic History of the Mexican Empire, 1861-7. Together with the Imperial Correspondence. With Portrait, 8vo. price 10s. 6d.

Madame Récamier, Memoirs and Correspondence of. Translated from the French and edited by J. M. Luyster. With Portrait. Crown 8vo. 7s. 6d.

Plutarch's Lives. An entirely new Library Edition, carefully revised and corrected, with some Original Translations by the Editor. Edited by A. H. Clough, Esq. sometime Fellow of Oriel College, Oxford, and late Professor of English Language and Literature at University College. 5 vols. 8vo. cloth. 2l. 10s.

Social Life of the Chinese: a Daguerreotype of Daily Life in China. Condensed from the Work of the Rev. J. Doolittle, by the Rev. Paxton Hood. With above 100 Illustrations. Post 8vo. price 8s. 6d.

The Open Polar Sea: a Narrative of a Voyage of Discovery towards the North Pole. By Dr. Isaac I. Hayes. An entirely new and cheaper edition. With Illustrations. Small post 8vo. 6s.

The Physical Geography of the Sea and its Meteorology; or, the Economy of the Sea and its Adaptations, its Salts, its Waters, its Climates, its Inhabitants, and whatever there may be of general interest in its Commercial Uses or Industrial Pursuits. By Commander M. F. Maury, LL.D. Tenth Edition. With Charts. Post 8vo. cloth extra, 5s.

Captain Hall's Life with the Esquimaux. New and cheaper Edition, with Coloured Engravings and upwards of 100 Woodcuts. With a Map. Price 7s. 6d. cloth extra. Forming the cheapest and most popular Edition of a work on Arctic Life and Exploration ever published.

"*This is a very remarkable book, and unless we very much misunderstand both him and his book, the author is one of those men of whom great nations do well to be proud.*"—Spectator.

The Black Country and its Green Border Land; or, Expeditions and Explorations round Birmingham, Wolverhampton, &c. By Elihu Burritt. 8vo. cloth, price 12s.

A Walk from London to John O'Groats, and from London to the Land's End and Back. With Notes by the Way. By Elihu Burritt. Two vols. price 6s. each, with Illustrations.

" No one can take up this book without reading it through. We had thought that Elihu Burritt's ' Walk to John O'Groat's House' was the most perfect specimen of its kind that had ever seen the light, so genial, lively, and practical were the details he had brought together ; but he has beaten his former literary production out of the field by this additional evidence of acuteness, impartiality, and good sound sense."—Bell's Weekly Messenger.

The Voyage Alone; a Sail in the " Yawl, Rob Roy." By John M'Gregor, Author of " A Thousand Miles in the Rob Roy Canoe." With Illustrations. Price 5s.

A Thousand Miles in the Rob Roy Canoe, on Rivers and Lakes of Europe. By John M'Gregor, M.A. Fifth edition. With a Map, and numerous Illustrations. Fcap. 8vo. cloth. Price 5s.

The Rob Roy on the Baltic. A Canoe Voyage in Norway, Sweden, &c. By John Macgregor, M.A. With a Map and numerous Illustrations. Fcap. 8vo. Price 5s.

NEW BOOKS FOR YOUNG PEOPLE.

TORIES of the Gorilla Country, narrated for Young People, by Paul Du Chaillu, author of " Discoveries in Equatorial Africa," &c. Small post 8vo. with 36 original Illustrations, 6s.

" It would be hard to find a more interesting book for boys than this."— Times.

" Young people will obtain from it a very considerable amount of information touching the manners and customs, ways and means of Africans, and of course great amusement in the accounts of the Gorilla. The book is really a meritorious work, and is elegantly got up."—Athenæum.

Life amongst the North and South American Indians. By George Catlin. And Last Rambles amongst the Indians beyond the Rocky Mountains and the Andes. With numerous Illustrations by the Author. 2 vols. small post 8vo. 5s. each, cloth extra.

" An admirable book, full of useful information, wrapt up in stories peculiarly adapted to rouse the imagination and stimulate the curiosity of boys and girls. To compare a book with ' Robinson Crusoe,' and to say that it sustains such comparison, is to give it high praise indeed."— Athenæum.

The Marvels of Optics. By F. Marion. Translated and edited
by C. W. Quin. With 60 Illustrations. Cloth extra. 5s.
   " *A most instructive and entertaining volume, comprising not only a
   carefully-written and popular account of the phenomena of vision and the
   laws of light, as illustrated by the latest discoveries and experiments of our
   wise men, but a history of ' Natural Magic" from its earliest to its latest
   wonders.''*—Observer.

Also uniform.
Thunder and Lightning. From the French of De Fonvielle, by D. T.
   L. Phipson. With 38 full-page Woodcuts. 5s.

Alwyn Morton ; his School and his Schoolfellows. A Story of
   St. Nicholas' Grammar School. Illustrated. Fcap. 8vo. 5s.

The Silver Skates ; a Story of Holland Life. Edited by W. H. G.
   Kingston. Illustrated, small post 8vo. cloth extra, 3s. 6d.

The Voyage of the Constance ; a tale of the Polar Seas. By
   Mary Gillies. New Edition, with 8 Illustrations by Charles Keene. Fcap.
   3s. 6d.

The Boy's Own Book of Boats. A Description of every Craft
   that sails upon the waters ; and how to Make, Rig, and Sail Model
   Boats, by W. H. G. Kingston, with numerous Illustrations by E. Weedon.
   Second edition, enlarged. Fcap. 8vo. 3s. 6d.
   " *This well-written, well-wrought book.*"—Athenæum.

Also by the same Author,
Ernest Bracebridge ; or, Boy's Own Book of Sports. 3s. 6d.
The Fire Ships. A Story of the Days of Lord Cochrane. 5s.
The Cruise of the Frolic. 5s.
Jack Buntline : the Life of a Sailor Boy. 2s.

The True History of Dame Perkins and her Grey Mare, and
   their run with the Hounds. Told for the Countryside and the Fireside.
   By Linden Meadows. With Eight Coloured Illustrations by Phiz.
   Small 4to. cloth, 5s.

Great Fun Stories. Told by Thomas Hood and Thomas Archer
   to 48 coloured pictures of Edward Wehnert. Beautifully printed in
   colours, 10s. 6d. Plain, 6s. well bound in cloth, gilt edges.

Or in Eight separate books, 1s. *each, coloured.* 6d. *plain.*
   The Cherry-coloured Cat. The Live Rocking-Horse. Muster Mis-
   chief. Cousin Nellie. Harry High-Stepper. Grandmamma's Spectacles.
   How the House was Built. Dog Toby.

Great Fun and More Fun for our Little Friends. By Harriet
   Myrtle. With Edward Wehnert's Pictures. 2 vols. each 5s.

A Book of Laughter for Young and Old.

A Bushel of Merry-Thoughts, by Wilhelm Busch. Including the
   Naughty Boys of Corinth, the Children that took the Sugar Cake, Ice
   Peter, &c. Annotated and Ornamented by Harry Rogers, plain 2s 6d. ;
   coloured 3s. 6d.

Under the Waves; or the Hermit Crab in Society. By Annie
E. Ridley. Impl. 16mo. cloth extra, with coloured illustration   Cloth,
4s.; gilt edges, 4s. 6d.

Also beautifully Illustrated :—

Little Bird Red and Little Bird Blue. Coloured, 5s.
Snow-Flakes, and what they told the Children. Coloured, 5s.
Child's Book of the Sagacity of Animals. 5s.; or coloured, 7s. 6d.
Child's Picture Fable Book. 5s.; or coloured, 7s. 6d.
Child's Treasury of Story Books. 5s.; or coloured, 7s. 6d.
The Nursery Playmate. 200 Pictures. 5s.; or coloured, 9s.

Golden Hour; a Story for Young People. By Sir Lascelles
Wraxall, Bart. With Eight full page Illustrations, 5s.

Also, same price, full of Illustrations :—

Black Panther; a Boy's Adventures among the Red Skins.
Stanton Grange; or, Boy Life at a Private Tutor's. By the Rev. C. J.
Atkinson.

Paul Duncan's Little by Little; a Tale for Boys.   Edited by
Frank Freeman. With an Illustration by Charles Keene.   Fcap. 8vo.
cloth 2s.; gilt edges, 2s. 6d. Also, same price,
Boy Missionary; a Tale for Young People. By Mrs. J. M. Parker.
Difficulties Overcome. By Miss Brightwell.
The Babes in the Basket: a Tale in the West Indian Insurrection.
Jack Buntline ; the Life of a Sailor Boy. By W. H. G. Kingston.

The Swiss Family Robinson; or, the Adventures of a Father and
Mother and Four Sons on a Desert Island. With Explanatory Notes and
Illustrations. First and Second Series. New Edition, complete in one
volume, 3s. 6d.

Geography for my Children.   By Mrs. Harriet Beecher Stowe.
Author of "Uncle Tom's Cabin," &c. Arranged and Edited by an Eng-
lish Lady, under the Direction of the Authoress. With upwards of Fifty
Illustrations. Cloth extra, 4s. 6d.

Stories of the Woods ; or, the Adventures of Leather-Stocking :
A Book for Boys, compiled from Cooper's Series of "Leather-Stocking
Tales." Fcap. cloth, Illustrated, 5s.

Child's Play.   Illustrated with Sixteen Coloured Drawings by
E. V. B., printed in fac-simile by W. Dickes' process, and ornamented
with Initial Letters. New edition, with India paper tints, royal 8vo.
cloth extra, bevelled cloth, 7s. 6d. The Original Edition of this work
was published at One Guinea.

BELLES LETTRES, FICTION, &c.

DAVID GRAY; and other Essays, chiefly on Poetry. By Robert Buchanan, author of " London Poems," " North Coast," &c. In one vol. fcap. 8vo. price 6s.

> " *The book is one to possess as well as read, not only for the biographical essay on David Gray,—an essay of much more than deep interest, of rare power, and a strange unimpassioned pathos,— but also for certain passages of fine original criticism, occurring in essays— thickly sprinkled, we admit, with foreign substances—on poetry, and the religion and aims which modern poets should put before them.*"—Spectator.

The Book of the Sonnet; being Selections, with an Essay on Sonnets and Sonneteers. By the late Leigh Hunt. Edited, from the original MS. with Additions, by S. Adams Lee. 2 vols. price 18s.

> " *Reading a book of this sort should make us feel proud of our language and of our literature, and proud also of that cultivated common nature which can raise so many noble thoughts and images out of this hard, sullen world into a thousand enduring forms of beauty. The ' Book of the Sonnet,' should be a classic, and the professor as well as the student of English will find it a work of deep interest and completeness.*"—London Review.

English and Scotch Ballads, &c. An extensive Collection. De- signed as a Complement to the Works of the British Poets, and embracing nearly all the Ancient and Traditionary Ballads both of England and Scotland, in all the important varieties of form in which they are extant, with Notices of the kindred Ballads of other Nations. Edited by F. J. Child, new Edition, revised by the Editor. 8 vols. fcap. cloth, 3s. 6d. each.

The Autocrat of the Breakfast Table. By Oliver Wendell Holmes, LL.D. Popular Edition, 1s. Illustrated Edition, choicely printed, cloth extra, 6s.

The Professor at the Breakfast Table. By Oliver Wendell Holmes, Author of " The Autocrat of the Breakfast-Table." Cheap Edition fcap 3s. 6d.

> " *A welcome book. It may be taken up again and again, and its pages paused over for the enjoyment of the pleasant touches and suggestive passages which they contain.*"—Athenæum.

The Guardian Angel: a Romance. By the Author of " The Autocrat of the Breakfast Table." Second Edition. 2 vols. post 8vo.

Bee-Keeping. By " The Times " Bee-master. Small post 8vo. numerous Illustrations, cloth, 5s.

> " *Our friend the Bee-master has the knack of exposition, and knows how to tell a story well; over and above which, he tells a story so that thousands can take a practical, and not merely a speculative interest in it.*" —Times.

The Rooks' Garden, and other Papers. By Cuthbert Bede, Author of " The Adventures of Mr. Verdant Green." Cheap Edition. Post 8vo. cloth, gilt edges. 3s. 6d.

The White Wife; with other stories, Supernatural, Romantic and Legendary. Collected and Illustrated by Cuthbert Bede. Post 8vo. cloth, 6s. Cheap Edition, fancy boards, 2s. 6d.

Queer Little People.   By the Author of "Uncle Tom's Cabin."
Fcap. 1*s*.   *Also by the same Author.*

The Little Foxes that Spoil the Grapes, 1*s*.
House and Home Papers, 1*s*.
The Pearl of Orr's Island, Illustrated by Gilbert, 5*s*.
The Minister's Wooing. Illustrated by Phiz, 5*s*.

Entertaining and Excellent Stories for Young Ladies, 3*s*. 6*d*. each,
cloth, gilt edges.

Helen Felton's Question: a Book for Girls. By Agnes Wylde.
Faith Gartney's Girlhood. By Mrs. D. T. Whitney. Seventh thousand.
The Gayworthys. By the same Author. Third Edition.
A Summer in Leslie Goldthwaite's Life. By the same Author.
The Masque at Ludlow. By the Author of "Mary Powell."
Miss Biddy Frobisher: a Salt Water Story. By the same Author.
Selvaggio; a Story of Italy. By the same Author. New Edition.
The Journal of a Waiting Gentlewoman. By a new Author. New Edition.
The Shady Side and the Sunny Side. Two Tales of New England. By
Country Pastors' Wives.

  " *Written with great power, and possesses a deep and captivating in-*
terest—an interest which will enchain the interest of all contemplative
readers.   We remember nothing in fictitious narrative so pathetic; we
wish such books, and especially this book, to be read by everyone."
                                                          Standard.

Marian; or, the Light of Some One's Home.   By Maud Jeanne
Franc. Small post 8vo., 5*s*.   *Also, by the same Author.*

Emily's Choice: an Australian Tale. 5*s*.
Vermont Vale: or, Home Pictures in Australia. 5*s*.

            Each Volume, cloth flexible, 2*s*.; or sewed, 1*s*. 6*d*.

Tauchnitz's English Editions of German Authors.   The following are now ready:—

1. On the Heights. By B. Auerbach. 3 vols.
2. In the Year '13. By Fritz Reuter. 1 vol.
3. Faust. By Goethe. 1 vol.
4. Undine, and other Tales. By Fouqué. 1 vol.
5 L'Arrabiata. By Paul Heyse. 1 vol.
6. The Princess, and other Tales. By Heinrich Zschokke. 1 vol.
Other volumes are in preparation.

LONDON: SAMPSON LOW, SON, AND MARSTON,

CROWN BUILDINGS, 188, FLEET STREET.

English, American, and Colonial Booksellers and Publishers.

Chiswick Press:—Whittingham and Wilkins, Tooks Court, Chancery Lane.